Heni

Robert Dalby and his World of Troubles

Being the early Days of a Connoisseur

SALZWASSER
VERLAG

Henry Merritt

Robert Dalby and his World of Troubles

Being the early Days of a Connoisseur

1st Edition | ISBN: 978-3-75255-536-3

Place of Publication: Frankfurt am Main, Germany

Year of Publication: 2022

Salzwasser Verlag GmbH, Germany.

Reprint of the original, first published in 1866.

ROBERT DALBY

ROBERT DALBY

AND HIS

WORLD OF TROUBLES:

BEING THE

EARLY DAYS OF A CONNOISSEUR.

PHILADELPHIA

1866.

CONTENTS.

ROBERT DALBY.

CHAPTER I.

THE ORPHAN.

THE Universities of Oxford and Cambridge are equally remarkable for crooked streets, dark lanes, and out-of-the-way thoroughfares in which poor people linger out their lives, secure alike from prying dons and insolent students. On this account, therefore, I shall have no fear for the incognito which it is my intention to preserve. Such localities as I may have occasion to describe in the following narrative will be found to exist in common in either University.

Friars' Lane, or Chequers Yard, as it was more commonly called, consisted of a row of old tenements forming one side of a narrow court, situated in the suburbs of one of the seats of learning in question, out of sight and forgotten by all save a few inveterate antiquaries—who forget nothing that is old and decayed save poor old men and women. Of all the members of the collegiate foundations around, only one poor sizar, an object of charity himself, was ever known to enter Friars' Lane, so that we had the place well-nigh to ourselves and lived quiet lives; for the most part in keeping with the gloomy aspect of the houses, which by reason of their great antiquity had become encrusted with moss. Silvery grey and sombre green, woven, as poets would write, in dark sunless hours by the hidden fingers of Time. The worn broken pavement telling of much traffic in days past, had also become clothed with the same mysterious texture of age. A high wall, which was meant to, and did effectually, shut in Friars' Lane, also excluded the sunlight from the inhabitants, save just one hour's burst at mid-day. At the end of the Lane were the town ditch and fortifications, and through a cavity in the wall, which would have been repaired had it been known to the authorities, we commanded a glimpse of the county jail, a massive tower and dense keep, old as the Normans; a place where men had groaned in fetters for many centuries, and over whose frowning battlements crimes unnumbered had been expiated on the gallows. Before six years had passed over my head I had beheld executions for sheep-stealing, arson and murder, and become familiarised with these horrors. The lonesome ways of the poor inhabitants of this dismal neighbourhood failed, however, to create any very unpleasant impressions on my mind.

Looking back to my first recollections I know that my home was in the fields. I call to mind a little room with a bed and curtains white as snow—the windows open, and on the sill and up the sides of the casement vine leaves and tendrils: it was in autumn time, for on a table spread with a napkin lay a heap of ripe grapes newly gathered. I remember little else. Fruit and sunlight in the foreground, with a background very dismal: another room wherein was placed a coffin.

I first entered Friars' Lane, which I have described, by night. I was carried there by an old woman: an old man with a lantern led the way. The old people were my grandfather and grandmother. I was an orphan.

CHAPTER II.

PRIMITIVE INFANT SCHOOL.

In neighbour Mistress Vane's Infant School I early became a pupil, where things went on pretty much in accordance with the reputation borne by these humble establishments. Mistress Vane was no great stickler for formalities: it was rarely that anything like order was preserved among us. The boys did pretty much as they pleased. Some of them exhibited no little ingenuity. One, a wiry shock-headed fellow, would beguile the morning with a lump of clay, shaping it into bricks upon the boards; another would divide his dinner into a number of morsels and spread out a miniature feast before a dozen imaginary guests, who, however, were not at all required to assist the owner in disposing of his meal. One owned a piece of string, of which he made many uses—among others, in imitation of the jail people, to hang a doll belonging to one of the girls. The champion of the boys, however was distinguished by the possession of a knife, with which he cut his dinner and anything else that offered itself to his notice, so that in the end there was hardly a thing in the room that he had not cut. He even had the temerity to reduce the length of the governess's wand. Most of the children were too poor to have anything about them save the garments in which they stood upright: yet though their pockets were empty, they took immense pride in having pockets, and spent part of their time in turning them inside out, in a triumphant way, to the envy of those who had none. The boy with a piece of string was considered fortunate: the brick maker with his lump of clay not badly off; but, greater than a king, he of the knife kept his ground against all comers. The knife was the very wonder of the establishment, and it was seldom out of sight or out of mind. Being a good-tempered urchin, the possessor of this instrument seldom drew blood from others, but hacked and chopped his own fingers until they were like a saw, and Mistress Vane was generally engaged with her sticking plaster on his special account. There were however times when we were not permitted to trifle with the governess. There were prayers and hymns to be got through by rote, and cards of the alphabet and words of one syllable to learn. One of the injunctions with which Madame reluctantly troubled us, was that we were on no account to disfigure the cards. Notwithstanding this, I am obliged to own they soon took a sickly hue and gradually dwindled away: from a square they became oval, and eventually, nibbed and nibbled into no manner of shape, disappeared altogether.

CHAPTER III.

THE SCHOOL BROKEN UP.

UNFORTUNATELY for us all, Mistress Vane and her school were of brief duration. A few months, possibly a year, passed by, and the governess and her school and everything belonging to her vanished from human sight; disappeared as if through the trap-door of a theatre. The paraphernalia of her teaching-room, the white wand, the rush-bottomed chair; all sank and left not a wreck behind. Winter came and nipped her sorely. Her end was so lonely and strange that I well remember it. One night my grandfather missed the accustomed gleam of light from the bow-window, and straightway a thought came into his head.

"Emily," said he to my grandmother, "I have not seen a light in the old governess's window this evening."

"And who knows," said my grandmother, "but

that the poor old lady is without the price of a candle."

"I should not wonder," mused my grandfather. If anything happened to her, I should not like her to be alone—I should not be able to reconcile it to myself."

"Give me a candle," said he abruptly. "We can spare a candle anyhow, and if we couldn't we would."

Being furnished with the lantern, my grandfather stepped out, and when he was under the old elm near the governess's door, he hesitated and listened: and, as he was attentively looking at the casement, a man came up and accosted him.

"Can you tell me if any one lives in yon bow-windowed room."

"I hope so," said my grandfather, struck by the question: "but why do you ask?"

"Out of curiosity. Passing a few moments ago I heard a tapping on the glass. I looked up but could perceive neither sign of light nor life and even as you now came under the tree the tapping was again repeated in the same strange manner."

Without making any reply, my grandfather, lantern in hand, ascended to the room of the governess and there found matters worse than he had expected. Stretched on her bed, still grasping in her hand the long wand--lay the poor old lady. Sensible to the last, and feeling her end draw nigh, she had thought by tapping on the window pane to arrest the attention of the passengers or haply of some neighbours. But alas, her efforts proved fruitless; she had sunk back upon her pillow, uncomforted by mortal aid.

CHAPTER IV.

THE LONG FROST.

THE historic event known as the "Long Frost" occurred when I was about six years old. The sexton of St. Margaret "did a deal of business that winter" in the back churchyard, for the mortality was chiefly confined to the old and poor. There were a class of poor who would on no account "go into the House," that is the Poor-house, and what was more, would not receive "Out-door relief." The authorities scraped together a considerable sum of money, but in those days, as now, mechanics were loath to receive paupers' funds. They could work for hire, but would not receive the wages of charity. This difficulty the wealthy citizens tried to overcome. There was a large tract of idle land in the suburbs, on which, far as the eye could reach, not so much as a bush (not to say hut or shed) was to be seen, to afford shelter to man or beast. Pleasant in summer, its dainty carpet of daisies and clover fed innumerable horses and cows:

in winter it was half covered with ice, owing to the prevailing autumn floods. It was an ingenious idea of the sheriff and bailiff who had charge of that icy region to take the opportunity of a well-stocked labour market, to dig a dyke and throw up an embankment to keep the swollen river within bounds. Those who could dig but would not beg were sent in gangs to work in that region of desolation. Poorly clad old men took pickaxes and spades, and set out each morning with empty stomachs to dig and delve. They tied ragged handkerchiefs round their mouths to keep their toothless jaws still, but their peaked noses took the purple hue of starvation; and their shrunken cheeks became blanched with want. The place seemed like a picture painted by some Polish artist, of the barren region of Siberia, only that, in place of Cossack overseers, the gangs were directed by worthy aldermen and sheriffs, well protected from the cold by stout overcoats and woollen comforters without and old ale within. Distinguished by his lofty stature and by his skill with the pickaxe, my grandfather stood among that band of amateur navigators, doing the work of a score for the pay of one. Not a word of complaint fell from his lips. There were others more wretched than he. His whole life had been passed in labour of the severest kind. From youth upwards he had been chiefly employed to build scaffoldings for masons and often ran terrible risks.

I have seen him climb the giddy height, when he seemed but a speck to me high up in the sky, stepping from pole to pole and from plank to plank. It was said that he was the best scaffold builder in those parts. But who thinks about scaffold builders ! We see a belt of planks framed around the steeple and ask no questions how it got there. We see a man carrying poles and planks up ladders planted on ladders, two hundred feet from the ground ; he pauses, seats himself on the slippery pole, splices, binds and wedges the rickety structure into shape, and tier rises above tier until the gilt vane in the clouds is reached. A terrible calling that of the poorly paid scaffold builder ! My grandfather built scaffolds for more than forty summers almost unharmed, and in the end met the fate of a dog.

He came home from the moors one Saturday at dusk with his "bit of money ;" and it was a bit. It was Christmas-eve, and grandmother had gone all the way to the wharf for some coals, for which she paid one shilling and threepence, being at the rate of five shillings a hundredweight. She made a fire, and got some trifle on credit to put in the pot against the old man arrived. He supped by the light of the fire to save candles—no great hardship that. It might have been nine o'clock. I was in bed and asleep, when a terrible groan startled me awake.

"Get up, my boy, get up," cried my grandmother. 'Your poor grandfather is very ill. Go to the grocer's and get a rushlight. What a thing it is not to have a bit of candle! Good God, what shall I do?"

"Let the child lie in his bed," said my grandfather. "It will give him his death to send him out in such a night as this."

"I shan't be gone five minutes," said I, starting up and slipping on my clothes.

"Ah! I am afeard thee won't get served," said my grandmother. "Being Christmas-eve, the place will be crammed up to twelve o'clock."

It was as my poor old guardian surmised, the shop was full. Gathered about the counter stood a number of town people and college servants chatting with the grocer and his assistants, who took no more notice of my order than if a cur had barked in the street. Oh, that I had then possessed a little of that shrewdness which adversity has since taught me! Will any one believe me when I say it, that it never struck me to go to another shop for my candle? But then I was only six years old. With desperate efforts I made ever and anon for the counter, and called out, "A penny rushlight, if you please, sir." All in vain. I was elbowed by the fat college servants and gyps. Then would I shrink back in silence and endure for a time such agony of suspense as I have never since felt. I tried the master, I tried the dainty assistants, I tried the porter, all equally in vain. Large orders came tumbling in, and I had in every instance to give way to my betters. At length the clock struck twelve, and the place became almost vacant. Only three old stagers remained, determined to empty a bottle of brandy with the grocer before they sought their homes. Now again I rush to the counter, for they were rattling up the shutters, and preparing to close. At length my tremulous voice took effect. The porter heard me.

"God bless my soul!" he exclaimed, so as to be heard by the others, "if I don't believe this poor boy has been asking for a candle three mortal hours by the clock."

"A splendid order," said the college butler.

"Will cause a rise in tallow," observed the grocer's assistant.

"May be," said the porter, in an under tone to the foppish assistant, "that the boy may prove as good a customer as some of the best of 'em to-night. At least he pays for his candle, while some of your dons who order a cartload of goods take a world of credit, and some of 'em never pay at all;"—saying which he handed me the candle.

It was snowing hard without, and with what I had endured and the terrible cold of the night I became almost paralysed. It was barely possible for me to find my way, notwithstanding that my visits to that detestable grocer had been frequent. I had no little trouble in threading my way home. At length I got into the lane, and gained the bed side of my dying guardian. There was fumbling in the dark for the tinder-box and matches, and after due time the cheerful light dispelled the gloom; but oh! trouble upon trouble, I held in my numbed hand only a wretched morsel of paper which had contained the rushlight, but the rushlight itself was gone—lost in the snow. I stood breathless a moment until the match expired. A groan escaped my poor grandfather, and in another moment I was in the lane and the street hunting on my hands and knees for the lost candle; but, alas, to no purpose. Sometimes I ran wildly about to and fro; anon I walked at my accustomed pace, and, muttering to myself, forgot all about the candle. Then I crouched under a tree and tried to be still, and then my lips blubbered up involuntarily, and I sobbed aloud. And there, cowering in the darkness, a death-like chill crept over me, my eyes grew dim, and gradually and irresistibly helplessness fell upon my limbs. Some little consciousness remained, and images of home rose up; my name sounded in the blast, and then I heard music in the air and all around. It was Christmas-eve to all the world, and college bells and church tower and steeple rung out merry peals, and well-to-do people steeped their toast in spiced wine and ale, gathered about blazing fires, and laughed and sung in response to the merry bells without. Meanwhile darkness, death and despair filled the home of my childhood.

CHAPTER V.

THE FUNERAL.

In summer time the churchyard of St. Margaret's was a favourite resort of children, who watched the sexton ever and anon as he came with pickaxe and shovel and lowered at last the parish dead one after another into their graves. At the season of which I speak, the mounds, the tombs, and black yew tree, were laden with snow, when the sexton came and cleared a place for my grandfather. Four masons' labourers, old friends of my late guardian, came from a long way off, and carried him to the spot prepared to receive his coffin. Grandmother was confined to her bed, so I and little Lucy, a chairwoman's daughter, were the chief mourners. The chairwoman took us in charge. Little we knew or felt of the sorrowful nature of the event in which we played so prominent a part. The grave was dug in a remote, obscure spot of the burying-ground, at the back of the church—a place gloomy and sunless as Friars' Lane—where the grass grew coarse and rank; a cold, chilly, dismal part, where the boys seldom went to play even in summer. The four labourers set down the coffin. It was very light, "no weight at all," they said, "considering." The parson was a long time in coming to perform the service, which delay seemed not to astonish the bearers. They sat down upon the coffin. A number of common idlers (Old Joe the parish idiot was one) came and looked on, as they would at any diversion, and laughed and joked as though they had something to laugh and joke about. One of these roughs played and tormented Old Joe, and threatened to bury him instead of my grandfather, which made the poor wretch cry like a child. By and by the parson presented himself at a back door. When we returned to the grave I and Lucy went close up and looked down upon the coffin, and Old Joe stared about him and grinned like an idiot, as he was.

CHAPTER VI.

THE DOG-FANCIER.

AMONG the coffin-bearers at my grandfather's funeral was a young man, who was related to the chairwoman previously mentioned. His name was Ben Jones. He had started in youth as a mason's labourer, but, having a wild and roving disposition, he had got tired of carrying hods of mortar and took to the woods for support. Out of six years he had spent three in the county jail for the offence of poaching. Such, notwithstanding, was his known good-nature that, regardless of his repeated appearance before the same bench, and which moreover boasted several clergymen, he managed to get off lightly; and although he once broke a saucy keeper's head, he had hitherto escaped being transported. Of all his fancies the love of dogs was predominant, and once on the death of a favourite pup, which he had tramped sixty miles to procure, he fretted himself almost into a decline.

I remember that he got a poor limner to paint a post-mortem likeness of the ugly little beast, and that he stuck the animal against the wall, in a favourite attitude, while the painter seized "the points." Ben had expected great things of the pup in question. Its mother had borne a good name, and its father was never known "to open," when hunting in Squire Blackmore's warren. Somehow or other Ben contrived to live on the best. He had fish and game in season, and he always had a shilling to spare a companion in distress. Yet Ben's resources were not wholly derived from nefarious sources. On the contrary, he carried on a legitimate business under the very eyes of the University authorities. He had a cottage on the banks of a canal, near a barge builder's, adjoining a brickfield, where he kept a number of valuable dogs for the undergraduates. And here also he kept hedgehogs, rats, and badgers on which to exercise the destructive tendencies of the terriers, bull, and other choice canines. If ever any one exercised a wholesome influence on Jones it was my grandfather, and at the old man's grave he wept like an infant. It was known to all but myself, while we were in the act of interring the veteran scaffold builder, that his loved partner, my grandmother, was in a state of insensibility on her way to the poorhouse. Ben knew this, and he also knew that I was destined to the same home of common wretchedness. The funeral over, the beadle came up to me, and in the kindest words he could muster took me by the hand and would have led me away; but seeing Ben, whom I had long known, I clung to his coat and would not stir from his side. The beadle coaxed and Ben urged, but all the more I cried and clung to the poacher.

"Leave go, will you," exclaimed Ben, getting vexed, but wiping his eyes at the same time; "go after your grandmother, will you." Scared by the beadle in his livery, and cane in his hand, I only roared the more, when all of a sudden the dog-fancier was inspired with an idea, perhaps the first of the kind he had entertained in his life.

"Why, what a fool I am," he broke out; "the lad will be worth his weight in gold to feed the pups;" saying which, and without more ado, he seized me by the "scruff" of the neck as he would a terrier, swung me under his arm and walked off, leaving the parish beadle in a stare of official bewilderment.

Of course the parish took no pains to find me out, and I entered in due course upon my duties as pup attendant, administering medicines during distemper and teething times, holding the little brutes while Ben shaped their ears to the orthodox pattern, or bit off their tails to the prescribed lengths. I learned to handle rats as though they were kittens and became so taken up with the kennel that I found no time to weep over my early woes.

It was a lonely spot where Ben lived, by the canal side, in a hut made out of an old barge. He often left me at night, and came home himself at daybreak bespattered with mire. For myself, I soon learned to be alone, and slept sound, for I had a dozen guardians at my beck and call, all ready to start up at the slightest approach of danger. In term time, Ben never went out at night, for he was busy with the students, who came by scores to look at new dogs, or take their own for a ramble, and one and all were kind to Ben and to me, and I often got a shilling given me, for extra pains taken in washing and combing the dogs, or displaying dexterity in grabbing the rats or "tackling" the badger.

Sometimes we smuggled a bag of rats into a college. There were a class of students then, as now, who never read themselves, and did all they could to prevent their fellow students reading. This class had some difficulty in finding objects of amusement. They got weary of tormenting poor scholars who wore spectacles and darned stockings, and who loved study for its own sake, and who were compelled to study whether they liked it or not, in order that they might be able to command the means of living in the future. The roystering students feared the University authorities in about the same degree as my master Ben feared the gamekeepers. Tired of Ben's pit near the canal, they wished to have one of their own under the bursar's nose. They carried out their intention regardless how it would have fared with Ben and his adopted son, had they been detected on sundry November mornings passing half a hundred rats through a certain Gothic window which overlooked St. Bridget's Lane. A one-eyed gentleman commoner had loosened an iron bar to allow of the bag passing through with its squealing contents. Some such dialogue as this I have often heard take place between my protector, standing in St. Bridget's Lane, and his patron at the casement.

BEN: "There, your honour, I think you will find them in stunning condition," forcing in the bag of rats.

GENTLEMAN COMMONER: "Ah, you are a monstrous clever fellow, Ben, but don't come too near with that greasy jacket of yours."

BEN: "I think, your honour, that we shall manage to squeeze Black Bess and the Proctor (two terriers) through. They'll follow that boy anywhere, your honour; they loves the very ground he stands on."

On one occasion the precaution was taken of placing me under a bed with my rats and dogs while the gyp cleared away the breakfast things. This fellow hated us because his master had given Ben a parcel of clothes on which he (the gyp) had set his heart. He hardly dare tell the bursar of our sports, but he would mightily have liked to put the proctor on our track. While I lay concealed, scarcely breathing, with my dogs and rats, the servant, mechanically employed in washing the cups and saucers, was calculating what he might probably realize by the "broken bits." "That pigeon pie," he remarked audibly, "will do duty again." (The crust had been removed in a piece). "I shall take out half a pigeon and put a whole one in with fresh gravy, and stick on the crust; the pastry-cook will allow me something for it. Then here's a knob of butter, three commons at least, three brown loaves and two penny 'busters,' with some coffee and four eggs, which is cold and not much account." With these observations the thrifty gyp stooped down and placed his spoils under the very place where I was, and left the room. Ben taught his sporting dogs silence, a desirable accomplishment when in echoing woods on the look-out for rabbits: but their master had never taught them not to eat when food was thrust in their way, and, do what I could, it was not in my power to persuade Black Bess from demolishing the pie and butter; Proctor, being the weaker party, contented himself with the rolls and eggs. My principal enjoyed the story amazingly when he came to hear it, and so did the gentleman commoner to whom Ben related it second-hand.

As I have said, we did well in term time. In the long vacation Ben spent a good bit of his leisure at the ale-house. A few miles off the canal passed a dense wood, and Ben would often set out to it at night with his gun and his dogs, leaving me with certain instructions respecting his establishment in case he happened not to return. One very dreary morning at daybreak, Proctor and Black Bess came home alone. They slunk in and began whining. I thought they asked for food, and threw them their usual allowance. They refused it, and kept on whining as before.

"Hang the dogs," I cried. "What can they be after?" I thought they might be ailing, and put brimstone into their pan of water. The matter was cleared up at mid-day by the arrival of a down barge. Ben had been watched, attacked, captured and put into jail on a charge of poaching, and disputing with violence his lawful capture. The report soon spread, and before night the entire kennel had disappeared. As previously arranged, the proprietor of a rope-walk carried off the whole establishment. Luckily for the rope-maker, I was there to interpose my authority, otherwise he might have found the task of removal no easy one.

CHAPTER VII.

THE ROPE-WALK.

The rope-walk whither Ben's dogs and plant were conveyed was familiar to me. A long narrow slip of land, bounded on one side by the canal and a thick hedge-row on the other, formed the united estates of the dog-fancier and the rope-maker. It was now my duty to turn a wheel used in rope manufacture. The whole of the dogs, save the two favourites known as Black Bess and the Proctor, were deposited with or sold to a fancier much in vogue with the students.

In my new occupation I sat in all weathers in a shed turning a wheel, whistling in mournful wise, or humming tunes which I picked up from day to day. Rope-makers sing and whistle all day long. At intervals I had to stir a cauldron of pitch and tar, a mixture used for tarpauling and coal-heaver's string. I made myself very happy in the shed devoted to the cauldron, roasting my potatoes or toasting my meat and cheese, as the case might be: sleeping among the dogs in the hemp at night. There was something very snug and inviting in the odour of the tar and pitch—and very wholesome too. There was a belief at that time that the smell of tar was good for asthma, and in cold weather we often had visits from old gentlemen troubled with phthisicy coughs, who came to inhale the fumes of the cauldron, deriving, as they fancied, great relief therefrom. Even people of distinction, members of the University, sometimes looked in for this purpose, for coughs were not confined to the poor and needy, though most prevalent among them. Thus it came to pass that in a few months of hard weather I picked up money to the extent of seven shillings. Ben was captured in autumn, and the assizes did not take place till March, so that he had to lie in jail all the winter, and I went now and then to take him a steak or bit of tobacco: but the bulk of whatever money I got I saved till the assizes came round to aid in engaging counsel, and this I did in consequence of hearing my master, the rope-maker, conversing with friends of Ben on the subject. But in spite of all we could do, Ben was found guilty, and sentenced to hard labour for two years. I now lost all manner of chance of seeing him again during all that time. For days I sat ruminating, while turning the wheel, which I had acquired the habit of doing mechanically; all the time my thoughts were with Ben in his prison cell. What could I do for him now? Who would give him steaks and tobacco now?

CHAPTER VIII.

AN ORDER FOR THE HANGMAN.

One day as I sat thus thinking one of the jailers from the Castle came into the walk. He was a good-natured fellow for a jailer, and talked with my master on Ben's position, and not without feeling, for in common with all who came to know him, he was grieved that a fellow of such genial qualities should have been so cursedly apt in getting into scrapes. I know not why, but it seemed to me that this jailer looked on me with a friendly eye, as I sat watching him. His errand was a strictly official one; and not of a pleasant character. There was a man to be hanged, and he had come to order a rope for the occasion. A farmer, in good circumstances, had out of malignant spite set fire to a neighbour's home-stead, and had managed to be, as he thought, very cunning in the matter, so that on his examination before the magistrates the evidence of his guilt was extremely slight. It was said that so certain was he of an acquittal, that he had on his way to trial actually ordered a dinner to celebrate the event. He happened, however, to be a lame man, with a peculiar limp, and certain tracks discovered in the soft clay, in the neighbourhood of the arson, proved circumstantial evidence against him so strong that he was condemned to death. While I sat turning the wheel I thought that, should it fall to me to be sent with the rope to the Castle, I might, perchance, find means once more to see and speak with the incarcerated poacher.

It was so. Before daybreak I set out on my way with the fatal coil swung over my shoulder. It was a windy March morning, and rain and sleet came down in blinding showers. My way lay along the canal, and owing to the darkness, I had much difficulty in keeping the narrow path; and to make matters worse, the rope seemed to cling to my side, and weary me. Each huge, gaping drawbridge on the way groaned hideously, and overhead leafless pollards stretched out their scraggy arms. Every object which, one after another, became discernible, seemed a frightful shape. Yet the thought of seeing my old master gave me courage, and I kept up well on my journey. Day broke by degrees, and over the leafless hedgerows, willows, and fields the sun threw a sort of amber-tinted light. Familiar objects stood forth, familiar sounds rung harshly out, and boatmen passed to and fro, with hasty strides, on the tow-path and wharves, who seemed to scan with curious eye me and my burden. Perhaps this; perhaps the fulness of the day, now fairly dawned, threw me into a reverie. During the making of the rope much had been said of executions, and of particular ropes which had been used in recent times, which my employer and his father before him had manufactured, and of which pattern specimens had been carefully preserved, nailed up in the shed, where I sat by day, and slept by night. Many stories, too, were told, and dreadful incidents cited, in which ropes were the principal features, not omitting the silken cord which had suspended a noted earl in times long gone; and thus my thoughts ran wholly upon the horrible thing whose weight well-nigh bore me down. The farmer for whom the rope on my shoulder was intended was a remarkably clean man, with white hair, and when I beheld him in the court he wore a neckcloth white as snow. Considerately enough, when I would have rested the rope upon the soddened ground, I was deterred from doing so by the remembrance of this fact; and exerted myself in order to avoid soiling the rope. It will seem perhaps incredible, and yet I was that affected by the influence of personal cleanliness, which, when exhibited even in a criminal, remains a virtue to command respect.

At length the Castle, with its awful towers, its keep and moat, appeared before me. In the presence of these familiar objects my mind shook off its load of sombre thoughts. There was Friars' Lane, near at hand, among whose inhabitants I still numbered friends. Daring and strength revived. I reached the gate and rung the bell that summoned the jailer. It was the friendly jailer's face which appeared, and in a moment I had passed the ponderous barrier, and was in the outer yard of the castle, where preparations for the execution were going on. The jailer's son was playing merrily near the lodge. He had gone to Mistress Vane's school, and we soon renewed our acquaintance. He sprang up from the step on which he was, and insisted on sharing my burden with him, and thus a procession was immediately formed. The jailer led the way, the rope-bearers followed him to a corner of the yard where a hearse was in waiting, and the carpenters engaged putting the gallows and drop in order. In those days friends were permitted to remove the bodies of culprits after being pronounced dead by the jail surgeon, and hence the presence of the hearse. The carpenters were assisted by prisoners, with whose strange garb I had become familiarised, but I had not succeeded in picturing to myself the sort of figure Ben might possibly present in the uncouth motley, and therefore I failed to distinguish him among the convicts. Not so with a voice at my elbow, which I at once recognised.

"Are you happy master?" I asked, in an undertone.

"Pretty middling, my boy. Black Bess and Proctor, all right?"

"As sound as a rock, but frets a little."

"Where do you hang out o' nights?"

"I sleep along with the dogs in the shed, all very comfortable."

"Gets your tin at the rope-walk all right, I suppose?"

"More than I want, master."

"More than you want, eh? Then just mind what I say. You know the elm tree over the wall, near the tower, on the keep yonder?"

"Every twig of it."

"Very well," says Ben. "You just come to-morrow night, and throw a ball of pigtail over the spikes in direction of that tree; it's just possible I may put my foot on it in the morning; and mind, if you keep your eyes open, you will often see me working on the keep; and, according as you notice where I work, throw from time to time a bit of 'baccy always under a tree near the wall. Don't pitch anything over but 'baccy; and now get out of this place as fast as your legs can carry you, and if you tumble down, don't stop to get up again;" saying which, Ben walked away to lend a hand in raising the fatal beam.

CHAPTER IX.

MARGARET TRENT.

It was in vain that my new companion, the jailer's son, pressed me to stay and see the execution. I followed Ben's advice, and got out of the jail-yard with speed. Not that I was afraid to see the hanging. In those days boys were not squeamish. Pugilistic encounters were encouraged among juveniles. Of the sports which then prevailed, bull-baiting and cock-fighting were the chief. In fact, on my way from the jail that morning, I came upon a large number of charity school boys who had been dismissed by their master for the day, in order that they might be present to witness the execution with a view to their moral improvement, a favour which they one and all seemed to appreciate vastly, most of them being in high spirits and playing at leap-frog to keep themselves warm.

About two hours before the time of the execution,

I was standing near an inn in the vicinity of the Castle where carriers' carts were accustomed to stop, when who should I see among the throng come into the town to witness the hanging but the dog-dealer to whom Ben's dogs and goodwill of his trade had been consigned, in earnest conversation with a rustic girl: known to us all as Ben's betrothed. The carrier's cart never brought into market town a more beautiful girl than Margaret Trent, nor, as it turned out, a more unfortunate one. She had come from her home amid the moors, expelled by her mother who could not reconcile herself to her daughter's persistence in her love for the convicted poacher. This disagreeable fact had been communicated to Ben before his trial, and he had arranged with the dealer in dogs, his successor in trade, that the proceeds of the sale should be paid by instalments to her whose misfortunes he had occasioned and whom he was powerless to succour. A great villain was the man in whom he confided this trust. Margaret had come into the city by his design. He had persuaded her that she might there best while away the lonely period of the poacher's imprisonment. As for the money, he would make arrangements for forwarding it weekly. My appearance proved opportune. I was chosen as well suited to fill the post of messenger. Margaret was borne down with grief, and only too willing to have come to her one whom she knew to be intimately connected with the poacher: and that I might be sure of the whereabouts of her lodgings, we all three went to the house where a single furnished room had been hired by the week in the most wretched neighbourhood of the whole city. Hooker's Hole consisted of a block of houses of ancient date, old as the Priory walls, which lay crumbling on the river side, close at hand. Here fishermen, poachers, dog-stealers and boatmen made their homes. Many dark alleys, and no thoroughfares existed thereabouts, adapted to every sort of vice. By day one would have regarded the locality without suspicion. The peaceful stream glided past, the fisherman sat mending his nets, and the bargemen lingered about pending another of those journeys which they called a voyage. Night was the time to be dreaded by the poor and virtuous few whom circumstances compelled to live in Hooker's Hole. Not that noise and tumult characterised the place. The rigid discipline of the University laws rendered prudence necessary, but the vice which abounded was not the less to be feared because it was pursued in silence and in the secrecy of night. The room selected for the reception of Margaret was in the house of a stout widow, who, in spite of her coarseness, was in some respects a good sort of woman. She received the girl and myself with very good grace, all things considered, and did everything in her power to cheer the rustic maiden, promising her what protection she could give her. She said many kind things and made many kind promises in a voice far from gentle, but evidently intended to be soothing: for great was the contrast when taking the dog dealer round the corner of the alley she informed him in tones that might be heard, and were evidently intended to be heard over the whole neighbourhood, that if he, the Bath Boy (such was the name he went by) did her new lodger, the poor country wench, any harm, either by word or deed, why then she, Mother Jones, would wring off his carrotty head. Mother Jones was well known to be a body likely to carry out her threat as far as practicable, and the Bath Boy seemed to respect the threat of the strong, muscular woman, for he protested that he never intended the girl any harm.

"May be not," returned the widow; "and now I think of it, let's have the first week's pay—four shillings and sixpence."

"With all my heart," said the Bath Boy, paying out the silver bit by bit very reluctantly.

It afterwards became my task to extract the like amount from him every week. It was not always easy to find my man, and, when found, not easy to get at his money: but my perseverance increased with the obstinacy of the debtor. His haunts were usually the tap-rooms of public houses, his pastime playing at all-fours for drink and coppers. He was always accompanied by several ferocious dogs and always in an ill-humour. On each Saturday night I haunted the Chequers, the Pheasant, or Blue Pig taverns. Waiting until nightfall, I approached the windows and peeped in, or listened at the door, and having satisfied myself that he was there, I boldly walked in and presented my claim. He would have set his dogs upon me but for the fact that Black Bess, my old friend, was ever at my heels ready to tear his best bull terrier limb from limb on the slightest pretext for so doing. Black Bess had a reputation in the respective tap-rooms of the town. The number of bulls she had pinned, the badgers she had drawn, and the rats she had extirpated made up a prodigious sum total; unmolested, she was harmless as a leveret, but in an encounter her bite was death. While I was absent from the rope-walk, Proctor, my other friend, kept watch and ward over the hemp and tar barrels, so that, whether at home or abroad, I felt alike secure. If my body-guard had one fault, it was the very natural one of a wolfish appetite. Yet even this vice was not a burden to me, for they were well known and caressed by every butcher and butcher's boy in the town, and had the entire run of several college kitchens. It was no uncommon thing to see them walk in at dusk with huge bones and pieces of cold meat, which they had no doubt come by honestly.

But to return to Margaret, she eked out her scanty income by mending and washing for two or three fishermen who moored their punts at Hooker's Hole quay. Sometimes the fishermen paid her in fish, and sometimes in cash, as their means permitted. Great was the respect borne by these hardy men for the unprotected girl in her solitary room, which I alone had liberty to enter. There everything was the perfection of order and cleanliness. When Margaret went abroad to make her trifling purchases, many eyes followed her movements; and but that prayers were unknown in the locality, many a prayer had been breathed for her safety. With a bearing almost ladylike, and a voice like the sweetest music, my ward, as I might term her, was unable to read or write. Now it happened that I, who had barely learned the alphabet and some score of words at Mistress Vane's academy, had become a tolerably competent reader. In the shed where I daily sat at the wheel, the boards were literally covered with songs, ballads and last dying speeches, pasted up by my various predecessors in the not very exciting occupation of rope-walk wheel-boys. By dint of hearing these said or sung, and comparing the printed with the vocal words, aided by my school acquirements, I became able to construe the—for the most part—flimsy trash. Among the ballads there were some pathetic love stories tunefully worded with which I stored my memory, and sung them as I sat at my wheel.

CHAPTER X.

MARGARET'S FATE.

Among the subjects on which Margaret would speak on my calls, Ben formed the chief. The poor girl lived on in the hope of seeing her lover at liberty, of becoming his wife and reclaiming him from his evil ways. Sometimes she would question me concerning myself and my little wants, which in her eyes were no doubt of a grave nature; for myself, I had become so accustomed to them that I felt quite puzzled what to do with a parcel she one night handed to me, consisting of coarse sheets, shirts and woollen socks. In many ways she showed her great concern for my comfort, and I grew so partial to her in return that without doubt I should have laid down my life in her defence, had occasion required. Often would she ask me to sing or read to her, and often we wept in concert over the troubles of the "Poor Fisherman's Boy," whose story formed, as I have said, the subject of one of my pet ballads. After listening to the mournful ditty beginning,—

> "Down by the low lands a poor boy did wander,
> Down by the low lands a poor boy did roam;
> By his friends he was neglected, he looked so dejected,
> The poor little fisherman's boy, so far away from home,"

she would take me in her arms, kiss the tears from my cheeks, promise to be my sister, tell me I should be her little brother, and that when Ben came out of prison we should all live together and never part again. On these occasions she would send me home to my shed with Black Bess at my heels cheerful, happy and hopeful with the prospect of pleasant days to come. But those happier days were never to come to Margaret. While I was battling with the vile dog-dealer for the pittance which was to support her, and singing my ballads or reading any little trifle that fell in my way, she was dying inch by inch. The whole neighbourhood knew it. The roses had long left her cheeks: her steps were no longer light as she passed over the wharf; she no longer found strength to eke out the trifle allotted her by washing and mending. I was singing now cheerily at my wheel in hope of the happy home to come, and knew not how ill she was. About midsummer she took to her bed, and I found myself for the first time an unwelcome visitor. In a short time the terrible Ranters got hold of her, they having been

and as I sat within a grove of elms that skirted the fields, I heard the remote bells and chimes in church and chapel tower. Sheltered from the blast within the hollow of a tree, I watched the leaves beating down in showers, blown hither and thither, now scampering pell-mell along, cutting, like living things, a thousand capers on the ground—now lifted up on high, now falling motionless at my feet as the wind storm raged or slumbered. I was interested, and my thoughts occupied in a new way. When spring came my post changed to a green lane adjoining a wild common that stretched away for miles. Deprived of my hollow tree, like the lambs, I found shelter and delightful warmth on the sunny side of a thick, double hawthorn hedge-row, ragged, neglected and wild, which divided the green lane from the sterile common—an embankment of warm sandy mould, rich and fertile, with here and there a dark mound of decayed leaves and heaps of rotten sticks and pieces of bark forced into uncouth shapes, and braced together by the blast. Here and there innumerable snails, with bright variegated shells made their homes; and as, day by day, the warm sun penetrated nook and cranny, they crawled out as if to scan the scene. Beauteous blades of grass shot up among the sunbeams, as it were in an hour, to tempt the dwellers in those hidden nooks. By and by the parsley spread out its leaves and all the sweetest flowers of the lane grew confident. The crumpled leaves of the cowslip and the primrose began to unfold. Sometimes the heavens were overcast, bleak and stormy: and then the little living things crept back to their thorny hiding-places, among the sticks and stumps, and the flowers closed up and left me sad as before. Then came April with its soft showers and misty, tearful skies, when amid parting clouds the lark sang his jubilant song.

But the lane below was always stored with wonders. Near a pool of water, in an unfrequented place, I found white violets among the grass, and on the border of an old dyke blue violets perfumed the air. For a while the secrets of this lane and all its riches were mine, and I was often so happy in it as to shed tears of joy. It had once been the refuse land of the populous town, and was now mostly deserted. On this common were ponds where efts and frogs basked in the stagnant water. Gipsies encamped in the hollows, and water-carriers and market-gardeners grazed their asses. On the sabbath the rag-tag of the slums came to play at pitch-and-toss, and fight their dogs and game cocks and one another. Nevertheless, my lane remained for a long time untrodden save by myself. At the end of it was a dismal field which for years had been regarded as forbidden ground, a dreadful place fenced in on all sides alike from man and beast. The parochial authorities even in those days were, it would appear, driven to their wits' ends to know what to do with the sewage of the ten united parishes over which they presided. Having filled all the back ditches and adjacent streams, and created a pestilence which half depopulated the city, they selected the gloomiest part of the suburban common land, and thus ended for a time the sewage difficulty. No living being was ever beheld on that spot during daylight hours; the very birds checked their flight in the air and flew in another direction. The skylark was never known to warble there. In course of years some new scheme was acted upon, and the old cart ruts to this spot became choked up, vegetation sprung into life, and when the time of wild flowers came their beauty seemed all the brighter in the privacy in which they blushed. So deserted and almost forgotten was that place that any one might have set up a right and title to those acres, without fear of awakening litigation. Things were in this vague and uncertain state when chance directed me to the place with the rope-maker's swine, and the spring was far advanced before any new comer arrived to dispute with me the possession of the Workhouse Lane, as the thoroughfare to my sylvan glade was called. But my pastoral reign was destined to a sudden and violent termination.

CHAPTER XII.

HOSPITAL SCENES.

One morning, when, like one of Virgil's shepherds, accompanied by my faithful friend Black Bess (the brave beast had all along been the companion of my solitary life), I drove my charge afield, I found the entrance to the lane partially fenced up and the lane itself in possession of a number of boys headed by their father, a hunchbacked, forbidding looking man. It appeared that the old man had long been on the look-out for a plot of ground where he might build a hut, and raise cabbages for the market: and his sagacity had told him that the workhouse field was likely to serve his purpose as capable of great fertility at little labour or cost. Upon receiving some sort of authority from the workhouse board, before which he had *too* often appeared in the character of a pauper, he had set to work in earnest. My arrival on the first morning of these unexpected operations drew upon me the attention of the whole family; and as the temporary fence offered little obstruction to Black Bess, she advanced upon the intruders with no sort of reluctance, followed by my charge and myself in quick succession. In addition to the old man and his boys, we encountered a huge, hungry cur, who, without any difficulty set the pigs squeaking and flying in all directions. Black Bess seemed for a moment undecided what to do, so sudden had been the attack; but at length, understanding how matters stood, she sprang forward in her own noiseless style—it was the work but of a few seconds, and the mongrel cur lay sprawling and howling in the dust. At the same instant I myself was assailed by one of the gang. I had just time to observe the old hunchback drive a pitchfork through the side of Black Bess, when I was knocked down by a bludgeon carried by one of the junior ruffians.

On the following morning I awoke in the county hospital; my head plastered and bandaged. It might have been mid-day when I awoke, a blinding sunlight filled all the place. Old men, some with crutches, some with sticks, and wearing night-caps, hobbled to and fro, all ashy pale and haggard: and on the beds were others of all ages equally out of condition. After a time of fear, wonder, and surprise, I closed my eyes again.

When I next awakened, I found an elderly

gentleman seated near my bed, regarding me with evident interest. With eyes half closed I managed to return in some way look for look. Presently, another gentleman came in, who I afterwards learned was the house surgeon, when the following conversation took place.

Surgeon: "This is the lad to whom I referred this morning when at breakfast. He was brought in yesterday morning with a broken head. He has been brutally treated by some rascals in the workhouse field. It appears that he was employed by Jackman the rope-maker, to mind swine, and found good feed for them in Workhouse Lane. Yesterday, the field and lane were taken possession of by old Willis and his seven boys, who set upon this poor orphan, and treated him as you perceive, and, it is said, killing his dog, in addition to scattering his pigs. Jackman gives the boy an excellent character, and is determined to prosecute the wretches for the assault, but, as no one witnessed it, it may be difficult to get a conviction. Perhaps it would be better to devise means to protect the boy in future, than to make a futile attempt to punish the brutal aggressors."

Old Gentleman: "It struck me while waiting your coming in that the boy might be useful at the Hall. Do you think that his stay here is likely to be long?"

House Surgeon: "No; a day or two at the

most;" saying which the doctor came to my side to ask me how I felt. To which I replied that I felt very hungry; and as I had not tasted food since the previous morning, this state of my stomach was not to be wondered at.

House Surgeon: "You have heard what this gentleman has said; would you like to go into service?"

Not knowing what to say, I remained silent. Attributing my silence to want of intelligence on my part, the old gentleman suggested a consultation with my friends, which rather diverted the surgeon, who had my history by heart, obtained direct from the rope-maker.

House Surgeon: "The fact is, Sir Anthony, the boy is an orphan, without a friend to advise him. The rope-maker, as I said, speaks well of him."

Sir Anthony: "From whom did the rope-maker receive the boy?"

House Surgeon: "The less said on that point, Sir Anthony, the better for the boy. Since, however, you kindly take an interest in him, you perhaps ought to know that his previous protector was a somewhat notorious poacher, who broke your keeper's head last autumn, and is in prison for that offence at the present moment."

By this time the party at my bed-side had considerably increased. An undergraduate, in whom

I recognised one of Ben's former patrons, had joined the surgeon conversing on very familiar terms. The undergraduate was an eccentric man. His success in his examinations was brilliant, to the astonishment of every one who knew not his habits. He spent his days as it were in the kennel, and vaunted that he never read, while the fact really was that his days of sport were also days of severe study. His sole companion was an old accomplished scholar, who had in youth taken honours and might have risen in the Church but for reasons unknown. These two were identical in taste—fast friends—they lived together and read together by day and by night. This was the secret of our undergraduate's success before the examiners. The moment the young gentleman saw me he remembered me, and inquired after my condition. Having ascertained the object of the conference with Sir Anthony, he proceeded in a rattling way to settle the difficulty, by providing for me himself. He told Sir Anthony that I was an old friend of his, that I was an excellent lad, and that the governor, his father, was in desperate want of a boy to be about the yard, and that he would undertake to introduce me at the Rectory as soon as I was able to stir. He added that next morning he would provide me with a letter to the governor, which would make all things square.

When my visitors had left the room, I found that

there had been several listeners as the conference was proceeding. Among them was, as fortune would have it, an elderly patient who had known my grandfather and who had gathered up certain little facts of my life since his old friend's death, which had touched him to the heart, and the result was the following dialogue.

First Old Man: "They 've got the poor boy a place some twenty miles off, but they said nothing about his getting there."

Second Old Man: "These fine folks mean well, maybe, but they never think of the difficulties of the poor."

Third Old Man: "Not they. It be ten to one the lad ain't worth a groat, to say nothing of a proper turn out."

First Old Man: "Nothing but the rags he came in with, and them be smothered with blood."

Second Old Man: "It 'll be a damnable shame to turn out the child in that way."

Third Old Man: "Old and feeble as I be, and I had that Dick Willis within arm's length, I'd be hanged but I'd play old Harry with him."

This conversation was interrupted by the nurse, who came with a pan of warm water and sponge to remove the marks of the contest from my head and garments. With the exception of my smock-frock and boots, I still wore my only suit, namely, a pair of corduroys and ragged shirt: the corduroys tied up with string, in default of braces. While pursuing her good work the kind woman learned what arrangements had been made for my welfare, and immediately made a suggestion of a highly practical nature.

NURSE (addressing old men): "Most like the lad will have some sort of livery, when he gets to his place; but it won't do for him to go such a scare-crow as he is; and now I come to think on't, I've a couple of striped jackets, and a couple of old shirts, that belonged to Bill, my poor boy, that died three weeks ago was a twelvemonth, from the kick of a horse." Here the nurse began to weep, and the old men turned aside their heads.

NURSE (continuing): "And now I think on't, why, I can make up the poor orphan quite a natty bundle. He'll want a comb and a brush, and a change of shirts and pocket hankichers."

SECOND OLD MAN: "And I'll give him tenpence, which I saved towards buying a coffin—a trifling matter, not worth a thought."

THIRD OLD MAN (an old servant): "And I'll give him a receipt for cleaning plate, which I've got in my box under my bed. It may be useful to him by and by when he gets to be under-butler. God knows, it's never likely to be o' use to me again."

FIRST OLD MAN: "And he may have my pocket-comb; for now my hair's all gone, what's the good of a comb to I?"

SECOND OLD MAN (addressing the patients generally): "Who's got a pocket-hankercher to give away?"

"I," said a feeble voice from the adjoining bed; "I've a couple of cotton uns, almost new. He can have 'em both. They ain't likely to be of account to I, for I be given over."

The several contributions were gathered together, the nurse undertaking to make up the bundle in due time, and to see that I had a good wash from top to toe, and that my hair was cut, and everything done to make me tidy.

At last a man came round, whom I was more glad to see than even the bundle so kindly improvised for me, and this was the distributor of the wooden bowls of broth, who brought me a good allowance, with a substantial piece of mutton in it, the effect of which was to finish my cure. In the course of the afternoon I felt so well that staying in bed became an impossibility on my part.

CHAPTER XIII.

THE BUNDLE.

A WEEK after the scenes in the hospital, described in the preceding chapter (my little matters were soon arranged at the rope-walk), I set out on my journey of twenty miles to take service in a gentleman's family. The various articles for my outfit were got together, washed and packed with speed, for, as the nurse remarked, "I had jumped into a good thing," and "a good chance must not be thrown away." I had hoarded up in the shed a heap of copper money, amounting to five shillings, and having nothing to spend upon clothes, I started in spirits, with minute directions as to the road and way-side alehouses, where to rest and obtain refreshment. By mid-day I had placed eight miles between me and the ancient University where I had graduated only in misfortunes. It was not without pride that I despatched my dinner beneath a spreading chestnut tree in front of a small inn, and there in an evil hour lent an ear to the stable boy of the inn, and became the dupe of that cunning rustic.

By his advice I tried a short cut, which cost me a night in the woods. Following a small path through fields, meadows, and lanes innumerable, I ended my day's walk in a lonely entanglement of trees. Feeling about among the shrubs, I found a large tree trunk, and there sat me down, with no sort of fear, for darkness had been familiar to me. Anyhow, nothing remained for me but to rest where I lay. I had strayed into a bed of fern, both dry and warm, and I had the judgment to wrap and entwine the foliage round my limbs, just as I had been accustomed to swathe myself in hemp on a winter's night in my shed. There I lay, with my bundle for a pillow, and began, according to my custom, to reckon up my days, and calculate upon a sort of future, until my reflections ended in dreams of Ben and poor Black Bess, cruelly slaughtered, as I had concluded, in the Workhouse Lane. I dreamt, however, that the brave dog still lived; that after the conflict, where the hunchback had driven the fork into her side, she had hidden in the dyke, and that her brutal assailant himself had come to her and gently carried her to his hovel; not out of compassion, but on account of the value of the dog, which, as I have said, stood high all over the town. Then I dreamt that the poor animal had managed, in the man's absence, to creep away and follow me, limping on the road, and that I took her in my arms and carried her until I was ready to drop with fatigue, and wondering what I should do with my charge at the Rectory, where I should hardly be permitted to keep a dog. While deep in this last difficulty, and much perplexed how to act, the night wore on, and my dream was suddenly dispersed by the double report of a gun. I awoke at once, seized my bundle, and tried to rise; but this was no easy matter. My ingenuity of the over night in tucking the long fern leaves under me had been effective; the leaves and stalks had become so interlaced that it required almost an equal amount of ingenuity to extract myself from the bed as it had taken to make it. While thus occupied, I had not perceived that I was undergoing the inspection of Sir Anthony's keeper, he whose head Ben had broken in the poaching affray. We recognised one another at a glance. We had met at Ben's trial. I stared at all around me with amazement. I had passed my night in a wood where the tall pines made night of noonday. The branches overhead were all alive and noisy with twittering, cooing birds, while long vistas between the trees were lit up with slanting sunbeams, and golden pheasants crossed to and fro among the branches, screaming as they flew.

Without speaking, the huge brute in velveteen strode towards me, and taking a cord from his pocket, tied my arms behind, and then proceeded to open my bundle, which he had an idea contained contraband goods; for keepers imagine that every bundle contains game. In a minute my anxiously-collected outfit was scattered in all directions, and all the solicitude of the kind nurse at the hospital rendered of little avail. Pocket-comb, striped jackets, white shirts and aprons were kicked about by iron-nailed boots without any sort of compunction. This was the second time I had been ill-treated, but now I had no one to help me. In my agony of indignation, had I had my liberty and means of revenge, I should not have hesitated to use them. But there was no help for it, and I had to witness the trampling of my things into the grass, leaving me nothing to wear at my new place; making me a beggar again, all through mean, malignant, petty spite; for by this time the fellow must have known that I was no poacher.

"Thee may think theeself lucky," he screamed, as he came towards me with a stick in his hand, cut on purpose; "thee may think theeself lucky that I let thee go with thee skin off thee back, and don't put thee along o' thy master, the damned rogue."

While he was yet speaking or screaming, his stick fell from his hand, and a huge black object passed me, and a horrible yell rent the air, and no wonder, for Black Bess—my faithful Black Bess—had got the keeper by the throat. It turned out that my four-footed friend had been found sleeping, or rather watching by my side; that the keeper had driven her out, and discharged both barrels of his gun at her; some of the shots had taken effect, but not seriously.

CHAPTER XIV.

THE RETREAT FROM THE WOODS.

FEAR, I suppose, lent me strength, or in my excitement I had loosened the cord with which the keeper had bound me, for to call off Black Bess and flee from the pine wood was with me the work of a moment. Of my poor bundle there was no time to think, much less try to collect. It seemed that the keeper was more frightened than hurt, for the moment the dog made away, he seized his gun and set about reloading it with great haste. What he meant to do with it I could only guess, for in next to no time my black friend was in the thicket, leading the way for his master, and it was fortunate for me that I found a guide so much to be depended upon. For a long time the dog kept up an even pace some yards ahead of me, looking back now and then, to be sure of my whereabouts. We often crossed paths, tracks made by woodmen, but never followed them.

If I slackened my pace the dog did the like. Towards mid-day I fell down from hunger and fatigue. I was starving, and saw nothing to eat —not so much as a berry. The ground was strewn with the dry leaves of the last year; for where I lay the blast came not. The leaves lay where they dropped, and so might I, for no one might find me in such a spot It was a pleasant place too, and I should have enjoyed it much under other circumstances. I repeated an old experiment, made often at Mistress Vane's school, that of putting a pebble in my mouth; and I found some relief to my stomach, and amusement for my teeth. I looked around, below, above; every tree was budding and blossoming, but nothing in the way of fruit or berry was to be seen—not so much as a crab-apple. I shifted my ground, and found a hawthorn bush, and ate a handful of its half-sweet, half-bitter leaves; I tore up some flags which grew in the neighbouring ditch, and having a good useful knife in my pocket, pared away the roots, and got to the core. I will not say that the root of the flag is very exciting food, but that and some water afforded me some satisfaction. Black Bess declined the flags and hawthorn buds, but helped herself to water. In fact, she seemed not at all hungry. No doubt she had supped over night on a rabbit. Having in some degree satisfied my own appetite, and feeling now by reason of the distance we had come, tolerably secure, I set to work to examine the condition of the four-footed poacher at my feet, and found about a dozen shot near the surface of her hind quarters, which I contrived to remove; for the knife I had in my possession was one given me by a nobleman at Ben's yard, which contained several curious instruments, with the use of which I was not unacquainted. My great concern was for the wound inflicted by the hunchback. The left hind leg of the poor animal I had seen all the morning dangled, and was well-nigh useless. I found a swelling which required the lance, which Black Bess, accustomed to my treatment, allowed me to use, and when, the limb being relieved, her foot could resume its place on the ground I was afraid that the grateful capering beast would bark right out with joy. She seemed wishful to show me that her action was as free and beautiful as ever. But our conversation still went on by looks and signs. My guide now led the way, and I had no other thought than that of following her—through a copse, the border of which we reached in a short time, and, looking through the hedge, I was not grieved to see a chimney of very rude construction, whence issued bright, blue, homely smoke. My sense of smell soon detected the grateful odour of pitch, with which the rope-walk had made me familiar. My ear recognised the creaking of the drawbridge. I was near the canal. The smoke came from the lock-keeper's cottage. Black Bess had made the journey before. There was quite an agreeable meeting between the old lock-keeper and the dog. I had not observed Black Bess leave my side, but such must have been the case, while I was looking out upon the cottage. I was surprised to see the incorrigible poacher bring in and place a fat rabbit on the hearth in a manner quite unconcerned. The catching of the rabbit must have been the work of a few minutes. Possibly, Black Bess's mouth being accidentally open, the rabbit jumped into it.

CHAPTER XV.

HOMELESS.

THE good offices of Black Bess and my old master's name secured me a meal at the hut of the canal lock. In the afternoon an opportunity offered itself of a passage in a barge to the wharf at Hooker's Hole, that unwelcome den of my city experience. But where else could I go? By midnight we arrived at the wharf and landed. All through the tedious hours occupied in the "passage" my mind had been sadly troubled. What explanation could I give of my return? Who would heed my account of the loss of the bundle? How could I face the nurse at the hospital? Nobody would believe my story. So I determined to be seen no more than I could help. Besides, that dreadful keeper would have his score to settle with me. I knew not the extent of the mischief Black Bess after all might have inflicted on his windpipe. Possibly no great harm was done to the fellow who was well muffled up about his throat. Still it was not a matter he would soon forget or forgive, and was hardly likely to let rest. On this account, I made my way to inner Hooker's Hole, where no keeper in those days dared to go—where I lay about till morning, when Mother Jones, Margaret's old landlady, gave me a corner, and with my capital of five shillings very slightly exhausted I provided a loaf and cheese for my own breakfast, and let out Black Bess to get one where she could, for the dog had plenty of friends in quarters questionable and unquestionable, as I have had occasion to mention before. By degrees as time wore on I left my hiding place; partly from taking courage and partly from restlessness, I began to go abroad. I paid a visit to Friars' Lane, called at the rope-shed by night to see how things were going on, and slept in some straw in a carrier's cart which stood at the back of St. Minfred's Church, in a gloomy place, little frequented by the towns-people. I was a vagabond to all intents and purposes. One morning, before it was well light, I found myself in front of the county jail, looking up the keep. Ben's occupation on the keep ended a few days after the execution, and hence I had ceased to carry the arranged supply of tobacco. My only comfort lay in looking forward to the day of his liberation — still five months off. It was a long time to wait, and when I thought of it my hopes fell: not that my prospects could be, after all, very bright in that quarter. My trouble was to get Black Bess off my hands, to tell Ben of Margaret's end and all about what she said and did. By and by I made acquaintance with boys similarly situated to myself, and we banded together for solace and self-defence, proving the truth of the old adage, "Birds of a feather will flock together." In our case the saying might have been true of birds without feathers, for some of us were sadly off for clothes. The police in those days troubled us not, for the simple reason that they had not been invented, and parish constables were pretty much harmless. The genius of each of our band contrived to find its suitable mode of expression. Some boys held horses at inn doors, others frequented the river bank, where boats were let on hire, or attended pigeon matches or fishing parties. A fisherman would adopt one, a poacher or a dog-fancier another —for these latter pursuits still had their followers: one thing only was certain, that no respectable citizen would permit one of us to cross his threshold.

I remember a circumstance occurring about this time, which now seems trifling, which then however annoyed me very much. I was leaning against a tree in a field, where the gentry and their families often came. It was a summer day, and a beautiful woman daintily dressed passed close by me, leading a little girl gaily attired. I know not why, but my eyes were instinctively drawn towards this little beauty. But scarcely did our eyes meet than she began to cry lustily. The mother looked dreadfully concerned, and cast a contemptuous and threatening glance at me.

"What's the matter, my pet?" she asked soothingly and coaxingly of her little charge.

"That naughty boy looked at me," whined the dainty little beauty.

"Naughty boy, go away! How dare you look at my little girl? Go away, naughty boy."

I said nothing to this foolish, ill-natured woman, but the impression she made upon me rankled in my mind. I was coward enough for some time to avoid the gentry after this encounter with the lady and her pet. I kept more in the slums, where I was as good as my fellows. And so the days wore on, the summer passed and autumn set in: and poverty too, for, in the absence of the students at vacation, I had fewer horses to hold, and many little trifles derived from attendance at rat-pits failed me. Nothing remained for me but to poach. There were, however, degrees in poaching, and I tried to keep within bounds. I sought only those places where the landowners were not game preservers, and consequently paid no keepers to watch. Fish and their habits were thoroughly familiar to me; I knew shelved and hollow banks where the barbel and chub lay in hundreds, to use the language of Job the Diver, "like horses in a stable."

CHAPTER XVI.

LOOKING FOR A CRUST.

It was at the end of August that our little band assembled on the wharf at Hooker's Hole to devise some means of getting a crust. As I have said, we were almost without clothes, and there was but one cap among nine of us. One wore shoes which were a great deal too large for his feet, and the consequence was that in any enterprise he was always behind. He of the cap succeeded better, because that article of dress often served as a bag to carry anything in which its owner chanced to light upon in an honest way. One possessed a tin saucepan which held water, but mostly served as a hat in emergencies of rain or sun. On the morning of the day in question our wits were almost at an end, when Saucepan, as we called him, suggested a mode of procuring a dainty meal. As we stood upon the bank of the river, we observed a fisherman empty cray-fish into the well of his punt. Straightway an idea was developed. We all ran into the river and commenced turning over stones and broken pottery and bones of animals in search of cray-fish. We succeeded in finding a great number, more especially in the holes of the banks and among the willow roots which grew along the margin of the river. It was good sport to dabble in the mud. When we had got a cap full we landed on an island, lit a fire, and there, with a halfpenny worth of salt thrown into the saucepan, we very soon transformed the dark-brown shells to the brightness of the scarlet berry and into morsels fit, as we thought, for the palate of a prince. Sometimes we went fishing, but this sport was too precarious. "No fish no dinner" was too often verified in our case. But even fish could be caught in the worst weather by those who could dive like a duck and keep under the water long enough.

There was a deaf and dumb man who lived in Hooker's Hole, called "Diver Job," who could catch a bushel of barbel and chub while the patient, shivering, blue-nosed angler on the bank could not get a nibble for the life of him. The season did not trouble Job, who dived down to the bottom of the river, crawled under the hollow banks and beheld the larger fish with their heads in holes like horses in a stable, as he said. He had a knack of seizing the large fish with both hands so that they became powerless to move, and, thus rising to the brink, Job threw his prey bounding on the shore until he had caught a shoal of them, and then tying the neck of his smock-frock he would put them in and march home in triumph. It was free water where we fished, and nobody interfered with us. I say we, for nothing pleased Job better than to be followed by a pack of boys whom he delighted to teach the noble art in which he stood alone against all England. The students patronised Job, and threw money in the river, which he speedily brought up from the bottom in his mouth. He threw somersaults which alarmed us, and, diving from the top of stunted willows, would disappear under the water, where he could remain until he was almost forgotten—and then turn up a long way off, where least expected. We lived on Diver Job for several weeks, eating up all the smaller fish which he threw on shore. When we got tired of Job and his fish, and Job got tired of us, and set in for hard drinking, we all came into town to subsist as we could on those miscellaneous opportunities which came so precariously and served us so ill.

CHAPTER XVII.

THE PRISONER RELEASED.

SULLEN October with its chill showers came at length, and the ponderous gates of the Norman castle were opened sufficiently wide to let out my old master Ben. It was fair-time, and all along the road in front of the castle caravans of wild beasts and theatrical stages were displayed: while on the opposite side, beneath the yellow and now frost-stricken elms, were placed drinking booths. Possibly at his own request, Ben did not leave the prison until it was dusk, for he was not one of those who made a parade of his delinquencies. He marked out his own course of conduct, and was prepared to pay the penalties he incurred. I had sat all day at the gate in company with the poacher's dog, cold, wretched and hungry, yet borne up by the prospect of seeing

Ben emerge into open air and liberty. He came at length, but with a look and manner which afforded little reward for my patience and watchfulness. In vain Black Bess assailed him with her caresses. He was very much altered. Barely speaking, he walked rapidly towards Hooker's Hole. Where else would a jail-bird go with any chance of obtaining a welcome? I followed as fast as my legs could carry me. We entered Mother Jones's door together, and found the widow preparing supper in anticipation of our arrival. She was as fond of Ben as she was of anybody, and looked upon him as a son almost. Ben scanned the brick-paved room. The lower orders have strange, queer ways: Mother Jones was so little affected at our arrival that she never so much as turned her head, but kept on with what she was doing. She knew Ben's step: he was come, and that was all she cared to know.

"What has made you so late, Ben?" she asked.

"I waited till dark that I might get away on the quiet. Where's Meg?"

"Meg?" cried Mother Jones, losing all composure at the mention of that name, and, turning full round, she said abruptly, "Dead and buried."

Ben looked at me as if he did not exactly understand what was said.

"It is true," I said; "she died last fall of the leaf."

"And we buried her like a Christian," added Mother Jones, thinking there was something soothing in that.

"Four of the fishermen carried the coffin, and six girls in white followed," said I.

"Buried her down in St. Stephen's, right under the elms," added a woman who was present.

"And everybody cried," said I. Ben was silent, and we seemed to think that there was some consolation in these details.

"What did she die of?" at length asked Ben.

"Of consumption, brought on by grief."

"Did the Bath Boy pay up regular?" inquired the poacher.

"Anything but regular," said the widow; "he owes for fifteen months out of the twenty-four, the villain."

"She was starved," cried Ben, in a raging, husky voice.

"It is false," retorted Mother Jones.

Again Ben looked at me for explanation. "She couldn't eat towards the last," I said.

"She had fish and flesh and fowl. Old Otter of Dinwell Lock sent her in a pike as long as my arm only two days before she went off," added Mother Jones, and she continued: "That boy there behaved beautiful to her."

"I knew that he would," said Ben.

"She was very fond of that boy," said the widow, particularising me again.

"Was she?" said Ben, and, eyeing me from head to foot, he said, after a pause, "We must get clothes for the boy, Mother Jones."

"Or he will soon go stark naked," said the considerate woman, "for he has neither shirt to his back nor shoes to his feet, and now the nights are getting cold."

"We will shake some money out of the Bath Boy," said Ben, "and buy him some clothes."

"You will have some trouble to do that with the Bath Boy," said the widow.

"Why so?" asked the poacher.

"Because he is transported," was the reply.

"What have you done with my gun?"

"You don't want your gun to-night?" exclaimed the widow, apprehensive.

"You need not be afraid that I am going out to-night," said Ben. "I intend to raffle the gun, to get some clothes for the boy."

"I am glad to hear you say so, for a better boy never wore shoes and stockings."

"And shoes and stockings he shall have," said Ben.

"I don't think I could wear them now," I observed.

"Oh, you will soon get used to them—but come

and have your suppers, will you, for the food is getting cold and good for nothing."

Here suddenly ended my experience of Ben, for during supper the conversation ceased, and soon after I fell asleep.

CHAPTER XVIII.

CONVERTED INTO A MARKET BOY.

HAD circumstances permitted Ben to carry out his wishes, no doubt he would have parted with his gun to clothe me, but this was not to be. An old woman, whom I came to call aunt, but who I believe was but a remote relative, adopted me only two days after the poacher's release from prison. The proceeds of the gun raffle carried the owner into his native village of Staffordshire, where he got superior employment in a quarry, and no doubt kept up his reputation as a dog-fancier.

The excellent woman who took to me had gone to much trouble to assure herself of my identity, which had become somewhat doubtful, even in the comparatively short period which had elapsed since my grandfather's death. She had come into the town to keep a market-stall and had occasionally met with those who knew all my history—how, from having had a home in Friars' Lane, I had become a shoeless vagabond, wandering about the streets: and this seems to have moved her pity, and left her no peace of mind. She set others to work to find me, not succeeding herself in that benevolent intent. First and foremost the parish constable appeared on the wharf making fruitless inquiries, because those of whom he sought information naturally put him on the wrong scent, thinking that he meant me no good. After a while my relative resumed the search on her own account. At first she, too, did not explain her object, and therefore fared no better than the constable, but by degrees her respectability got understood and I met her, and, after much parley, agreed to go to her cottage, and permit her to adopt me as her son, for, as she observed, she had "neither chick nor child."

Her first acts on my arrival at her home were to have my hair cut short, burn my clothes, give me a warm bath, a good supper, and put me to bed. These were perfectly salutary and necessary proceedings, but, little savage as I was, I did not like the abridgment of my liberty they foreboded. My new mother had proceeded to manufacture a bed for me, by taking a dozen yards of close, coarse canvas, which she converted into a suitable sack, and went to a neighbouring barn where the men were threshing, and filled it with the beards of the barley.

Little idea of a soft bed can be possessed by those who have only slept upon feathers—they should try barley beards, which do not clog and mat together as feathers, flock, and down do, but always keep in motion, shifting with every movement of the body, remaining soft and crisp at the same time.

With the assistance of a tailor who lived in the next cottage, a miserable, sleepless "wight," I was provided with clothes in a short space of time, and even while slumbering a shirt was, as aunt said, "run together," in a rough sort of way: and, in fact, two days had not passed before I was comfortably clothed from head to foot—socks, boots, smock-frock, felt hat, and cotton pocket-handkerchief; nay, even a pair of worsted gloves were provided for Sunday, in order to impart an air of respectability to my hands and to keep them from chapping and chilling on the Sabbath.

It need not be supposed that my aunt, as I called her, was perfectly disinterested in her recovery of the lost boy. No sooner was I equipped than she took me into the market and hooked a basket on my arm. It was my part of the business to carry home vegetables and tripe. For the latter article we had an excellent reputation, on account of the remarkable cleanliness of our establishment. Thus I had given up liberty for slavery: nor did my relative stoop to coaxing in order to reconcile me to the change. She had an idea, poor woman, that shoeless vagabondism had no delights; the market-boy thought differently, but some sort of consideration of which he was not wholly incapable prevented him hinting so. I went on all my errands for a time quietly and cheerfully, carried home little parcels each night, and never murmured for green fields and sunny banks and brooks. Sunday came, and I was sent to the church, which was only a stone's throw from our cottage. I was able to read, as I have said, and consequently was provided with a prayer-book. Along with a few other boys I was ordered by the sexton to ascend a narrow stair, which led up to the back of the organ, where barely a ray of light could penetrate. This loft had been an addition made by some ingenious churchwarden, as a means of stalling up the rougher lads of the parish during service. Some of the boys brought peg-tops, some marbles, some eatables in the shape of carrots, turnips, and apples, to say nothing of bull's-eyes and alicampaine. The scent of peppermint pervaded all the loft. The first Sunday I found my head jammed against one of those horrible Gothic ornaments, representing a fiend with his tongue hanging out, and his eyes leaving their sockets in the shape of a corkscrew. In the distance I could hear a monotonous voice, but could not make out what it said. The preacher was more audible, being near at hand, and I paid marked attention to the sermon. If I could not follow the argument, I could pretend to do so, and did make-believe most earnestly. Just, however, as the church was most hushed, a few minutes before the close of the discourse, some little wretch near me had the misfortune to drop his peg-top. The sound was ominously near me, and so it turned out, for in the twinkling of an eye the ash stick carried by the sexton fell upon my head: my eyes struck fire, and a terrible pain shot through my brain. I went home to dinner with a bruised lump on my head, the size of a small walnut. My aunt was very indignant at my ill-treatment, and threatened to patronise the church of the next parish for the future.

CHAPTER XIX.

ENEMIES TURN UP.

THE market days came round again, and things went smoothly on until one Wednesday morning, when the Hunchback, who has already been described as having reclaimed the Workhouse field, and half killed Black Bess, turned up with his pack of boys at his heels. He came into the market with a load of turnips. I knew mine enemy at a glance, but flattered myself that he would not know me. Scarcely had he set eyes upon me, however, than he pointed me out to his boys, a ragged and well-fed set, and as impudent as it was possible to be. They made no attempt in my aunt's presence to molest me, but contented themselves with making mouths. I took no notice, but went on with my work. Shortly after, I had to leave the market with some vegetables for a customer—a lady, who went on before, to show me the way to her house, "in order," as she said, "that

I might know another time;" but I had not proceeded far, before I was set upon by three of the junior hunchbacks, "might and main." Without ceremony one seized my hat, another upset my basket, a third dealt me a blow in the eye. In a moment, porters and butcher boys scented a fight, and rushing from all quarters formed a ring, and to see fair play. A burly youth in a blue blouse, and a steel by his side, sat me on his knee, and, chafing my hands against my thighs, prepared me for a regular battle. Another butcher did the same for my antagonist. Seeing the work before me, and smarting with rage and pain, all the lately-acquired varnish of civilization disappeared in a moment, and the vagabond only remained. I turned to my second and told him I could not fight in my smock and boots, for I had not been used to them. "Bravo," cried the bystanders, and in a minute my feet and arms were free, and I was sent into the circle under the impromptu cognomen of "White-headed Bob," and told to darken the young hunchback's "peepers." I did as I was told. The rascal tried to skulk away, but he was forced back and soon his naturally hideous face bore marks of still worse disfigurement, in honour of the careful training I had received from Ben in the kennel, and kept up day by day with the Hooker's Hole vagabonds. The hunchbacks could not fight the least morsel in the world, and I knew it. I challenged the whole of them by turns. Renewed "bravos" came from the throng, and another hunchback was forced forward to enable me to give further proofs of my cunning in fighting, when my aunt rushed in upon us, broke up the ring, pounced upon the two hunchbacks, and scattered the crowd in all directions —to use an old simile, even as the dreaded hawk might scatter a brood of harmless chickens in a farm yard.

CHAPTER XX.

THE HUNCHBACKS PUNISHED.

Of course, I had speedily to put on my smock-frock and boots, and my aunt walked me off straightway to the town-hall, accompanied by the lady, who had seen how the affray commenced. His worship, seeing the character of the applicant and witness, immediately granted a summons returnable next day against all the hunchbacks, that is, against the old man and his three sons. They were only tried for the assault, but the mayor told them that he had a mind to commit them for highway robbery with violence. He had no doubt, he said, that they were a pack of ruffians. It appeared that a gardener had overheard the father set on the sons to assault me, and thus he was included in the charge. The bench fined them ten shillings each with costs, or a month's imprisonment with hard labour. The fine was reluctantly paid by the elder for himself, no doubt out of the proceeds of the load of turnips which he had sold the day before, but he left his hopeful offspring in the jailer's care. The lady, our witness, was known to the mayor, and took occasion to speak to his worship very highly of my aunt and myself, telling him how I had been adopted after a career of privations, whereupon he became thoughtful and looked hard at me and then at my aunt, of whom he inquired whether I went to school, "because," said he, "the lad has a promising face, and might be made something better than a market-porter."

My aunt curtsied and replied, "that she had no doubt but what his worship advanced was strictly true; that she had only just got me off the streets and had as yet had no time to devise what was best for me."

"My good woman," said his worship, "I have a mind to render the lad a service, for his behaviour in the matter of yesterday has placed him in rather a favourable light in my eyes. He proved that he is able to take care of himself, and those who act thus deserve to be taken care of, for I have no patience with people who allow others to impose upon them without making all the defence in their power."

Some of the magistrates on the bench acquiesced in the Mayor's remarks, and his worship proceeded: "It fortunately happens that I have on hand at this moment a 'turn' to put a boy into the 'Brown

Coat School,' and if you are prepared to keep the lad in food, why then, the matter is soon ended. The lad will receive a good sound English education, and at the age of fourteen receive from the foundation sufficient money to apprentice him to a useful trade. I can speak well of the school, for I there received my own education, and I doubt not that it has retained its sterling character; in fact, the same gentleman still holds the mastership as in my time."

My aunt fell in with the mayor's kind offer without a moment's hesitation. It was the very thing she desired of all others. In fact she had been all over the town to beg a "turn" to place me in the selfsame school. Giving his worship many thanks for his kind interest in my behalf, my aunt took me home well satisfied with the result of our appearance in court.

CHAPTER XXI.

EXPERIENCE AT SCHOOL.

AT the age of twelve, therefore, I became a member of an antiquated charity school in the city, which was by some considered fortunate in having for its master a very severe, hard man; but this was not the opinion of the scholars. Those who chanced to be endowed with more than ordinary intelligence, managed to escape being flayed alive. Some of them turned up in after times as respectable mechanics, or here and there a small shopkeeper. Such as happened to be dull at first were flogged into a state of downright stupidity, while any who commenced their career in this school in a state bordering on idiotcy were unceremoniously killed off. This amiable monitor of my young days regarded me in the light of his pet scholar. Yet he would not unfrequently threaten "to cut me in two in the middle": or, by way of change, "to flog me within an inch of my life." It fortunately, however, fell out that he was so much engaged in operating on more deserving claimants that I got respited from time to time.

I need hardly say that the parents of the majority were extremely poor, for only the children of the very indigent would consent to be thus flogged for their good. It was the custom in this school to place the last comer in the last place in the last class, and thither I was conducted. This post had previously been occupied by a heavy lad from a neighbouring hamlet, who laboured under an impediment in his speech. The master was exerting himself in endeavouring to remove this rustic's defective articulation, when I took my place by his side. The word which accidentally turned up for testing the lad's powers of improved articulation, was "aisle," which he insisted upon confounding with "oil." The experiment was conducted in the following manner.

MASTER: "Aisle."

BOY: "Oil."

MASTER: "Aisle."

BOY: "Oil."

The master being armed with a long heavy leather strap, he dealt the unfortunate stammerer a blow on the back, or across the thighs, at every failure in repeating the word. The operation thus briefly described really lasted more than an hour; but still the lad persisted in calling "aisle" "oil." During this period he really must have received a hundred blows. I, who had nothing whatever to do with the matter, fell in for a few smart raps, which I attributed not so much to accident, or to any unfortunate proximity to the patient as to design. This experiment was repeated on the following morning, and for several mornings, without success.

The next incident was one which monopolized the attention of the entire school, and well-nigh led to a large demand for parish coffins. This same boy who gained the victory over the master in the matter of pronunciation was in the habit of coming to school laden with the produce of the garden, the field, and the wood. Sometimes he brought turnips and carrots, wild apples, or the more civilized productions of the orchard. Occasionally he brought birds' nests and young rabbits, and more than once he introduced even snakes. Not unfrequently these commodities fell into the master's hands and were confiscated. It mattered not what class of property was found in our possession, we were always relieved of it by the obliging master, who paid us in full in blows. We thus early acquired ideas of exchange and barter, which bore a strong resemblance to highway robbery. Bob, such was the stammerer's name, numbered among his aquaintances out of doors a lad who lived at a druggist's: and this lad had among other discoveries in his master's shop found what, deceived by the taste, he designated blue alum, but which was nothing more nor less than poison. Few would think that alum would be considered a great treat even by boys at a charity school, nor was it, but some of the lads were so badly off that nothing came amiss. "Is it good to eat?" was the eager inquiry which arose on all sides when anything novel turned up. "Is it good to eat?" was an interrogatory not intended to go the length of ascertaining whether the article in question was good eating, but merely whether it could be introduced into the stomach without danger to life; and this point being settled satisfactorily by either information or supposition, into the stomach it went. Thus, while no one pretended that alum was a treat, still, as it was accessible and not poison, and could be consumed quietly without attracting the master's notice, large blocks were consumed. Bob's "blue alum," as it was named, found a ready acceptance, and the consequence was, that on the third morning of my scholastic career a level half-dozen of the third class were seized with horrible pains. The master, who never stopped to inquire the cause of anything, commenced strapping us all round. The school rose with excitement: something strange had taken place and was making itself felt beyond all power of the strap to arrest it. The secret at length came out, medical remedies were administered, and the six boys lost a valuable chance of escape from the miseries of school life. Poor Bob, who had not tasted the blue alum, but had innocently introduced it into the school, was, when the fact was traced to him, beaten into a jelly for his share in the transaction.

CHAPTER XXII.

THE PICTURE MAGAZINE.

NOTWITHSTANDING the ill-treatment I met with at school, I contrived to thrive in my learning, and obtained in a short space of time the post of monitor. My success was due (so said my master), to my possessing an excellent memory. But the Rev. Dr. Shrewd, one of the visitors, came nearer the mark when he ascribed my proficiency to attentiveness. I early acquired the habit of reasoning on little matters which concerned myself, and came to conclusions respecting the condition of life in which I found myself, which differed from those taught me. From comparisons thus early forced upon me, I decided, for instance, that the sphere on earth of the very poor was no paradise. I further came to the conclusion that, if an opportunity occurred to better my condition, it would be no great sin to take advantage of it. I certainly foresaw that, in the event of my making any change, it must needs be for the better, seeing that I could hardly take a step for the worse. Sketching was destined to be the form my ambition was to take.

My first studio was in the attic of my aunt's rickety cottage—a place used as a store-room for those productions of the garden which fell in my aunt's way to deal in, and which were intended for winter use. Thus had I been no better inspired than some of the old Dutch painters (or some of our present English painters for that matter), I might have found subjects for my pencil in the prodigious carrots, parsnips, and onions, which lay in heaps around my easel. But my genius aspired to nobler subjects. As monitor at the school, I was in the receipt of an income paid by the foundation. Twopence weekly was not a large sum, but then there were a few perquisites and little presents from the boys which one could hardly resist. True, they were intended as bribes, and unjustifiably accepted as such; but one thing was certain—the boys were happier under my care, and made better progress than before. One of my scholars was the son of a college servant, who had enough and to spare of good diet, which came from the tables of the collegians. Another boy's father made brawn; a third toffey, and so on. These may be said to have represented the better-off members of the school. I found that, as a matter of course, each of these boys brought a trifle illustrative of his parent's occupation. I found, moreover, that the master himself had no scruples in accepting a jug of dainty soup, or dish of brawn; and that those who were thus enabled to sacrifice at the altar of the strap were flogged less frequently than other less fortunate lads—at least such was the case in term-time; in vacation, when the dons were absent, the offerings necessarily ceased, and the thrashings were again equally balanced. Sometimes I obtained a dinner in the mode I have described, and saved my twopence—the amount alloted for my dinner when there was no cold food in my aunt's larder. Sometimes, too, on my visits to the colleges I obtained a meal from the servants who knew me, and were kind to me, as many of them were. They have little snuggeries, those servants, "scouts," or "gyps," as they are called, where they assemble after dinner in the hall and sort the remnants of the feast. Cold baked meats are not amiss when they are the leavings of learned divines, who are usually men of discernment in matters pertaining to the table. Many a slice of beef thus obtained in my boyhood might have won the praise of an epicure. I mention these things just to show the means by which I was enabled to follow my bent in the matter of fine arts. My aunt's twopences, my weekly stipend of twopence at school enabled me to present myself every Saturday morning at the principal bookseller's shop in the city for my "Picture Magazine."

Were I in the poetical line, which happily I am not, I should certainly, at this stage of my narrative, take the course usually adopted by bards, and invoke the aid of some goddess before proceeding further. Full well I know that ordinary words will fail to give the faintest conception of the delight which I felt in the possession of the "Picture Magazine." And this joy was renewed weekly. There was the anticipation of the next number, which gradually increased in intensity as the purchasing day drew near. On one occasion I mistook the day, and paid my visit for the illustrated periodical on Friday. In the whole course of my life I had never before mistaken one day for another (the poor seldom do), and it was certainly a strange coincidence, that on that particular Friday only the parcel of "Picture Magazines" had actually come to hand. It was an unlucky coincidence for the bookseller, for ever after I repeated the mistake, and presented myself six or eight times in the course of each following Friday, in the faint hope that the parcel might have arrived; but alas, always in vain. He was a good-natured man that shopkeeper, he had always a smile for me. My little head (which by the way, sometimes subjected me to unpleasant observations because it was large) scarcely reached up to the counter where I deposited my penny, and, in a timid voice, asked for my "Picture Magazine." The good shopkeeper saw my anxiety, which arose from the fear lest the parcel had not come, or that some rich collegian had forestalled me, and bought my copy. There was no reason to fear the latter alternative, for I believe that, rather than disappoint me, his "old friend," as he took to calling me, of my weekly source of inspiration, he would have risked offending the all-potent vice-chancellor himself. Had such a calamity happened to me, why then these sheets had never been penned, for I verily believe that I should hardly have survived the disappointment.

At the time of which I am writing, engravings after the best pictures of the old masters were appearing almost weekly in the "Picture Magazine," and here I may observe that, in my opinion, no wood engravings of the present day equal those somewhat early attempts to transcribe the beauties of the old masters' compositions to paper. I shall not easily forget the particular Saturday when "Jacob blessing Esau," after Rembrandt, made its appearance. I have that identical cut before me now, while I am writing these lines. On that day I was trebly fortunate indeed. First, I met with my favourite old master Rembrandt, and secondly, the master at school had, in consequence of over-exertion in flogging a desperate boy, brought on his annual attack of lumbago a fortnight earlier than usual. It was a glorious day. I not only ran and read, I flew, and devoured "Jacob and Esau" with my eyes. Hard drinkers have been known to go long distances after an orgie, and find their circuitous and adventurous way back, and awake the next day in their beds, without being able to recall to mind a single incident which befell them on their journey home. I had but the faintest notion myself that I ran my head against a coal-cart; the collision passed as a mere trifle; at all events, I stayed not my course until I arrived wild and breathless at my attic studio with "Jacob and Esau" in my hand. My old aunt was then sorting potatoes to complete a larger order than usual. She happened to look up as I entered. Never shall I forget her countenance as she stood aghast. The colour left her face. As she stared, I was induced to raise my hand to my head to feel what on earth could attract the old lady's attention, when I discovered that my blonde hair was matted with blood. In the intoxication of my delight, I had got a contused wound above my temple, the marks of which I shall, in all probability, carry with me to my grave.

CHAPTER XXIII.

THE ERRAND BOY'S FLIGHT TO SCHOOL.

In addition to my attendance at school, I soon had also other duties to perform, hardly less irksome. For a weekly payment of one shilling and sixpence, I became errand boy to a small stationer, thus filling up every spare moment of my time between school-hours, my dinner, which I carried in my pocket, being not unfrequently eaten, as I passed to and fro to the colleges with my parcels at the top of my speed. Among my master's regular customers, was a scholar and divine—a fellow on one of the foundations, who, out of a small income, managed to keep a mother, and a sister:—the latter as beautiful as an angel. This gentleman borrowed oratorios of my master, and in his delightful simplicity, and without design, managed to give me more trouble than almost all the other collegians put together. Scarcely a day passed, without my having to visit this poor quiet scholar. There was one luxury, of which he had long wished to avail himself without stint. His position as a fellow of the college gave him the privilege of using the chapel organ, one of the most perfect instruments in the world. One difficulty only stood in the way of thus rendering himself perfectly happy—that was, he had seldom the means of engaging any one to blow the bellows. One day while discussing this difficulty, his sister cast her blue eyes upon me in such a way as to leave upon me the impression that something out of the common way was uppermost in her thoughts, and in which I myself was in some way concerned. A small three-cornered note to my master revealed the plot. I was selected to blow the organ bellows for the best of brothers. My master, with his usual promptitude and liberality, returned an immediate answer, placing my best endeavours at the service of his fair correspondent. The favourable response to her request reached the lady, as she sat with her brother at luncheon, at the window of a dark Gothic room over-looking the college gardens. Never shall I forget the expression of that face: never did I feel happier than in thus becoming the humble means of making happier one so good and so fair. Only St. Cecilia herself could have thanked me with so sweet a grace, as, handing me some fruit from the table, she requested me to go over to the chapel porch and there await their coming.

By the aid of a stool, I contrived to reach the handle of the bellows, and after a little practice was enabled to perform tolerably well the office of supplying the huge instrument with the essential element of wind. Straightway the vaulted roof of the chapel was filled with sweet music, and a soft small voice rose above the organ's swelling tones. The joy of the brother and sister was complete. It was a day in June, sunny and warm. The gorgeous stained-glass windows rained down a thousand bright and variegated tints upon the tesselated chancel floor, and lit up, as with an unearthly radiance, the famous altar-piece, where a fair woman with a neck of ivory, flushed face and streaming eyes, knelt at a tomb in a garden of roses. It was the Mary Magdalene, on the morning of the resurrection, as she appeared in later times to the rapt vision of an old Spanish painter.

The singer paused, the music ceased, and the lady appeared, as I thought, to censure me for my inattention. The picture had so engrossed my thoughts that I had unconsciously faltered in my indispensable exertions at the bellows. She, however, came not to censure but to thank me for the skill I had exhibited on the occasion, and to further arrange for another day. It was with some difficulty that I aroused myself to my ordinary frame of mind, for the old picture was before my eyes and in my thoughts. Had I not read, even then, of poor boys becoming great painters and of their being honoured by popes and emperors? And were not vague but alluring images floating in my brain? One of the conditions of art eminence was mine for certain—I was sufficiently poor. Giotto himself could hardly have started better in the matter of his finances: for at the moment of which I am speaking I was not, I believe, in possession of a penny piece.

My delightful dream of old masters and young genius, in the organ loft, was, however, suddenly and cruelly cut short. The last words of the lady had scarcely ceased when a message from the clock-tower informed me that at that particular moment my harsh preceptor at the school had taken his place at the desk, and had commenced calling over the names of the boys, in which, as a matter of course, my own would not be forgotten. A tremor ran through my whole frame, and well it might. It was a terrible moment for me. One, two! The clock of St. Margaret's had proclaimed the hour, and out of the forty thousand inhabitants in that old city not one could be found to dispute the accuracy of that quaint, faithful herald of the fleeting moments. What the Horse Guards clock is to the metropolis St. Margaret's was to Oxenbridge. The fact stared me in the face that I had to run almost for my life, nearly two miles, in next to no time; and desperate as I was, I made the attempt. In a few seconds I was in the quadrangle and through the porch. The porter just opened his drowsy eyes, as I passed apparently without touching the stones, like as a "Moll hern," all legs and wings,* skims over the moor and along the sedgy shore of the silent stream, taking many turnings and windings, but withal travelling with desperate haste, out of sight before the sportsman is well apprised of his presence, much less has time to take aim. Vagabond boys in every part of the city saw distress in my speed, and got in my way: now and then a dog would rush out from some entry or door-step and hang impedingly on my rear. Onward, however, I flew. The streets and lanes were narrow, crooked and dark; but I knew every inch of ground, I might say every stone, and was prepared for curves and angles innumerable. Twice I fell and scrambled forward as I got up. My cap with the red tassel in one hand, my task book ("The Chief Truths of the Christian Religion") in the other—onward I still ran. Now I cast my eyes up at the clock of some ancient tower, of which there were several in my route, hopingly—despairingly. Could I be doing the journey in no time? Would the minutes stay their unresting

* The heron.

course that I might still escape being "cut in two in the middle," or "flogged within an inch of my life," as the case might be? One clock, apparently at a stand-still, encouraged the hope which another, half an hour in advance, dashed furiously to the ground. The clocks spoke no comfort. Breathless, heated, tired, hungry, terrified, I at length reached that dreadful place of martyrdom—the school. Four steps—a long dark passage, I am in the barn or schoolroom. Barns and schoolrooms were in those days pretty much alike. Instead of the chatter which usually greeted me on my entering the school, all was still and silent with well-known expectation. As I opened the door, a barely perceptible whisper, a noise as of many persons breathing in their sleep fell upon my ear: and there the schoolmaster—the executioner, the ogre to whom parents used to hand over their children for punishment—stood before me—or rather I stood before him. The strap—the dreaded strap! a yard long, half an inch thick, with a slit in the end, curved high in the air, and, with a movement rapid as forked lightning, descended on my shoulders, over my chest, across my wrists; hissing, scorching, blistering, like a tongue of fire, licking off the flesh and boiling the very marrow in my bones.

On leaving school some three hours after undeserved punishment and degradation, poor Bob, whose own ill-treatment was still fresh in his memory, came and presented me with a nest of young blackbirds, which he had left at a shop near the school. Such were the only means he had of saying that he sympathized with me as I had often done with him under similar circumstances.

CHAPTER XXIV.

THE CHARITY BOY PAINTS A PICTURE.

BEFORE I saw the altar-piece of St. Margaret's Chapel, and six months before the appearance of "Jacob Blessing Esau," after Rembrandt, in the "Picture Magazine," I had made sundry violent essays to paint a picture, but always failed for want of a little practical knowledge in respect of the mixing of colours. These attempts usually ended in my throwing picture, colours, and brushes out of the window, which exhibition of temper took with my aunt amazingly, because, as the ancient dame said, it reminded her so of my father. In those days the patent flexible tubes had not been invented, and painters carried their pigments ground in oil, tied up in pieces of bladder, using a tin-tack to puncture it when colour was required for use, replacing the tack to keep the colour from oozing out when laid aside. Now it happened that a painter of portraits came down from London for the season, and, by way of inducing public patronage, stuck his own portrait in the window of a popular barber. To this circumstance I trace some of the difficulties I experienced. In the back-ground of the specimen portrait in the barber's window the artist had introduced an easel and a canvas, on which the features of an alderman were faintly indicated, "rubbed in," as we term it. There was also a table, on which lay a mahogany palette, with its complement of colours, brushes, and maul-stick. In contemplating this composition I took very little notice of the principal object. My whole attention was directed to the paraphernalia of the studio, so ingeniously introduced. The easel, palette, and maul-stick I mastered almost at a glance. By turning two or three nights into day, and by the aid of some fragments of an old box, I contrived an easel, burning holes for the pegs with a red-hot poker, and, I might add, burning my fingers at the same time and getting a frightful scolding from my aunt into the bargain. The palette cost me more trouble and ingenuity. I was not satisfied to have it fair and square. Oval was the orthodox shape, and oval I was determined to have it. But what material should I employ to construct it of?—this was of course the prior question. On this point the London artist afforded me very little clue. The nearest approach in point of colour of anything I could "clap my eyes on" was the cover of an old book upon which I lighted on rummaging among my aunt's old lumber—and this I forthwith appropriated. I had burnt a hole for my thumb, and had with infinite trouble shaped it to the true oval, when my venerable aunt returned from the market and apprized me that I had destroyed the cover of the only book she had ever set store by in her life, and which she had always intended to have had repaired, only that she had never been able to find a book-binder to her taste. I was very sorry, but there was no help for it. This discovery did not however make me more careful, for on the following day I appropriated the lid of a potato-bin for a panel, and forthwith proceeded to copy on a large scale the group of "Jacob Blessing Esau." And now my troubles began in earnest. The easel, palette, maul-stick, and brushes were complete (I had invested threepence in the latter articles); but in respect to the colours I was completely at fault. That the little round forms in the picture on show at the barber's were meant for colours I had no doubt; but whether they were tied up in a dry or moist state never once occurred to me. Anyhow, I decided to keep mine in powder. To this intent I again ransacked my aunt's old lumber for gloves of bygone days, and herein committed another blunder in mistaking bladder for leather. Could anything be more wearisome? I found that

I had to untie and tie these clumsy contrivances every time I wanted a morsel of colour, so that nearly all my spare time was consumed in that operation, and I had hardly any leisure for the more serious part of the business. I know not how long I might have blundered on in this way had I not by accident come to hear something of the mode employed by the London artist. I heard a boy say that he heard the porter of St. Margaret's say that he knew a man who knew another man "as was sitting for his picture to the London artist what lived at the barber's in Booth lane." I had a pupil at school whose father was a "gyp," or bed-maker, at the same college as this porter, and I used my influence with this lad to get him to ask his mother to persuade his father to induce the porter of St. Margaret's to set his friend to press that other man "as was sitting for his picture" to take an early opportunity to inquire of the London artist what he mixed his colours with and what he tied them up in. This rather extensive and complicated amount of machinery being set in motion, the answer reached me in the course of a week to the effect that the artist mixed his colours in oil with a palette knife on a slab of marble and tied them up in bladder, and got the colour out as he wanted it by pricking it with a nail, and so on. The mystery was further cleared up by the good-natured artist sending me a partly-used bladder of colour, with the label attached by way of illustration. Forthwith my white lead, ochre, crome yellow, ivory black, red lead, and prussian blue were ground in oil, tied up in bladder, duly labelled, punctured with tin-tacks, ranged in systematic order in my box, and everything went on smoothly for a time. Only one other difficulty remained: to wit, my attic was not sufficiently exclusive to contain the artist in his increasing importance.

Had means of display permitted, I know not to how many of my fellow pupils I might not have been tempted to show my amazing studio. One had gone as far as daubing in water colours an engraving of Richard the Third, but not one had any notion of the mystery of oil colours.

When everything was advanced with my copy after Rembrandt my aunt astonished me by a piece of criticism which disconcerted me at the time, but which I have no reason to think was much beside the mark. Chancing to come up-stairs for a rope of onions which some customer wanted, my "Jacob and Esau" caught her eye. I was engaged on Jacob's long beard as she came in.

"Well, aunt," I exclaimed, "what do you think of my picture?"

"Think, my boy!" she asked, "why what can I think of it? What would you have me think?"

"I don't know, aunt," I answered, not feeling much encouraged, as I thought there could be but one opinion, and saw no reason for hesitation in expressing it.

"Why, then," said she, "it seems to my dim eyes but a poor melancholy daub." And she continued kindly, "Come down, come down, and have your supper, for I am sure you have been up here long enough."

I was too hungry not to take the advice tendered me. The old lady was not devoid of intelligence and I clearly had not made any favourable impression upon her by my first performance in oil colours.

CHAPTER XXV.

THE DEBT COLLECTOR.

While I lived with my master Ben, it was part of my occupation to idle about the college gates and by-ways with dogs which had to be shown to the under-graduates—and in after time, namely, in my shoeless period, I often frequented the same spots, so that I had every nook and corner of the place by heart, as it were, and I could have found my way from college to college blindfolded. Thus, when I became errand boy I made short cuts and performed my commissions with expedition. By this means I had sometimes a half-hour at my disposal, and it would often take my fancy to sit down in some dark unfrequented nook and brood over the past or speculate on an imaginary future. My favourite resort was a zigzag lane formed of high black walls of great antiquity, which were varied only by a couple of back doors, which were never opened. It gave me vast pleasure to sit in summer time and contemplate the crumbling stones studded with gilly-flowers. The lane was as like a trench or groove in the earth, out of which arose lightsome airy towers, pinnacles, and spires, glistening with gilded vanes, the resort of grey-headed chattering daws. I was often attracted by glimpses of the college gardens, caught as I passed their dark porches. I would sometimes peep in at open chapel doors and feast my eyes upon painted windows and polished marble pavements: or I crept into halls and whiled away ten minutes among portraits of founders and benefactors. I was no longer a vagabond. On the contrary, the garb which I wore was a guarantee of my trustworthiness. I became known to all the porters and gyps as a responsible messenger, in the employ of a respectable shopkeeper. Among the under-graduates I was not always welcome, for my pocket usually contained a number of small accounts of long standing which my master entrusted me to collect as favourable opportunities offered. The first to whom I made application for money was a gentleman commoner who afterwards arrived at great political distinction. My master, or rather my mistress, for the wife always managed the money matters at the shop, sent me dunning, but neglected to qualify me for the occupation, so that when the true son of a nobleman laid the money before me I was unable to give him a proper acknowledgment. Thereupon, he took pen and paper in hand and instructed me so effectually in the matter that to this day I have had no reason to change the form of that receipt for any other. Many little troubles arose out of my debt-collecting among the under-graduates, for I became one of the most indefatigable duns in the University. I got access when an ordinary collector stood no chance, because no one suspected me, a mere school-boy, of the order to which I belonged, of possessing half the effrontery necessary for this occupation. I became what is called "a character." My habits had given me a wiry frame, and a constitution which would defy a Siberian winter. With a worn and, I suppose, from what was said to me, a somewhat old look, I yet possessed activity of brain and limb. I was precocious without being rickety, sentimental without being morbid, except perhaps for a brief time. My questions, answers, and business readiness seemed to create no little amusement among some of the collegians of a light and mocking spirit. The mildest would insist that if I were no older than reported, that I must have made good use of my time. An old fellow whom I had dunned almost to death, for eight pounds which he had long owed my master for stationery, told me that my head recalled vividly to his recollection the head of an old tutor of his youth. As this man was somewhat in his dotage, he in the end actually persuaded himself that I was the identical tutor referred to, and took, whether alone or before others, to addressing me as his "most venerable preceptor." The antique coxcomb made me indignant beyond bounds. Perhaps there is no worse habit than to be constantly annoying boys in this way. One or other perpetually calling me in the same strain gave at last a sort of consistency to this banter, which made a painful impression upon me, and I framed crooked ideas of myself, which haunted me at all times and made me sensitive by night and by day, until I took the resolution of escaping from the city of Gothic buildings and Gothic prejudices, which had almost refused me bread and shelter, and now wholly denied me peace.

CHAPTER XXVI.

THE CARICATURE.

My aunt turned out after all to be very poor—poor almost as the vagabond she had reclaimed. Three months' rheumatism kept her from the market, and in the end her money was all gone, so that the trifle I got by running of errands became necessary to our existence. Warm weather brought her round, and she resumed her post; but meanwhile I had been compelled to break up my studio; my brushes had become hard, my colours dried up, and my strong passion for distinction reduced to a feeble state. What was to be done? I lived on little more than twopence a day. Still, in the midst of famine a sort of art-love continued to hang about me, and all the pretty and quaint wonders about the city famous for its quaintness and beauty pleased me more and more, as older I grew.

In one of the narrow lanes right in the heart of the

city were a group of old houses built against a college chapel, to which they acted as buttresses. In one of these tenements lived an excellent French artist, a drawing-master, whose windows usually contained about a dozen pictures, done in lead pencil upon cardboard. Twenty minutes often fell to my lot between school hours and other duties in which to eat my dinner, and, not having a home available, I took my frugal meal in the streets, where I could gratify my eye at the Frenchman's window at the same time that I appeased my hunger. The pictures exhibited consisted exclusively of views of the chief edifices and pastoral country around, to me familiar all my life. It appeared to me truly astonishing how pencil and paper could be made so surpassingly attractive. A rustic bridge or ruined archway would hold me captive for the full period prescribed for my dinner. Perhaps, if the pictures had been of a more complicated description, they would not have enlisted my interest so strongly. From the first a sort of vague notion entered my head that I might possibly one day be able to do something myself in the same way. I had given up painting in despair, but I might succeed with the lead-pencil notwithstanding. Intently I gazed on each sketch, and anxiously noticed each peculiarity of style, and the more I looked the more my interest increased, and day by day the thought and hope of becoming an artist took stronger hold of me and became more firmly fixed in my mind. For a long period I daily took my stand at that window, and devoured each new production with no less avidity than I did my meal. I should have begun pencilling at the first, but in addition to my want of time there was my inability to procure paper or pencils. In the absence of practice, I therefore made progress in theory. The shop of the artist was secluded and seldom troubled with any other visitor, and the interior was so enclosed that no furtive glance of mine could penetrate the room. Hence it never occurred to me that my frequent visits might give annoyance to the painter. The display of drawings in the window might, so far as I knew, have been got up for me alone, so seldom did passengers disturb me at my chosen post.

One day, however, at the usual moment when I had taken my stand, and commenced inspection, a curtain within was hastily drawn aside, and lo! for the first time the painter himself appeared. There was an angry scowl upon his face, and he darted a sharp look at his humble, though obtrusive admirer, which made me tremble from head to foot. At the same time he placed in the window a most atrocious caricature. Perhaps I had not seen my face in the glass ten times in my life, but the resemblance was not to be mistaken. There stood the little brown coat charity boy, with an enormous piece of bread—

eating on both sides of his mouth simultaneously, and forming, on the whole, the most ridiculous counterpart that could be obtruded on my conscious gaze. Now, it happened that at school I had been making rapid strides. In arithmetic I had a score of superiors; in writing I was nothing remarkable; but my almost inspired replies to Dr. Shrewd, who came once a week to examine us in theology, went far to compensate for any deficiency in the aforesaid accomplishments, and on the very day on which the caricature appeared in public I had been promoted to the high rank of usher. My alarm, therefore, at the sight of the satirical portrait, knew no bounds, naturally bashful, and grown sensitive of late; still I kept my ground at the window, and stared up at the abominable libel for a few moments in a sort of stupor, never doubting that I should become the butt of half the boys in the town. The blood rushed to my face at the bare thought. I who had admired, almost idolized, the genius of this man, to become in return his victim! It was too bad. Did he know that I had just been elevated to power at school—made usher of eighty boys of my own age? The artist stood like a fiend mocking me. So I thought. I was mistaken. He had merely miscalculated the character of his pertinacious visitor. The uncouth garb, and ravenous state in which he had usually beheld me, had excited his prejudice. It had not occurred to him that a charity boy could have a spirit as high, and as aspiring in its way, as his own. A few moments caused him to repent that he had taken so much trouble to annoy me. He had anticipated from me some vulgar approval at his, for the nonce, thoughtless act, and he had the mortification to see tears streaming down my cheeks. At length I rushed away. That night I sought my bed in a state bordering on distraction. The caricature never left me. All night long I fancied I heard the boys jeering me, and one family of lads in particular, ruder than ordinary, whom I had often encountered, stopped my way in the street, and would not let me pass. In vain I tried to sleep. My character was gone. The place would soon resound with my name, and I should lose caste in the school. It was more then than now the practice with some artists to make money by etchings of well-known characters, such as cripples and dwarfs, which were sold in print shops for about a shilling a piece; and I was to become one of these poor wretches, and acquire a print-shop notoriety, doomed to be followed by the rabble, and be the laughing stock of brainless or thoughtless under-graduates. I might, perhaps, have some days' grace before the thing would become known. Could I do anything to induce the artist to remove the object of my annoyance. I could think of no expedient. I arose as usual with the sun went to school in due course, and performed my accustomed rounds; but when the hour of dinner came I need not say that I found a fresh place in which to spend my time. Far within a sequestered churchyard, removed from every eye, I sat down upon a tombstone and thought the matter over afresh. I determined to visit my accustomed haunt at dusk, and, having formed that resolution, I grew more content, and despatched my meal. Haply it might not be there. I made a vow that, if the enemy had been so far obliging as to remove the dreaded sketch from the window, he should never after be troubled with the original. In accordance with this resolve, I went again in the evening, and stood some twenty yards off. The lights were not yet placed in the window, and I could not decide whether or not the nightmare of my sleep was among the sketches. I approached stealthily nearer, until within a few yards, when the servant, putting the candles in the window, set all my fears at rest. It was not there. Relieved beyond description, I turned to go, when a hand grasped me gently by the shoulder. It was the artist himself, but how unlike the look he wore the day before! He was all compassion and kindness.

"My young friend," he began, "why have you not been to see my pictures to-day? I have been all over the city looking for you. I want to talk with you. I have wronged you. I will ask you to forgive me. Come into my house. You shall have tea with me." And thus he went on, taking away my very breath for wonder.

Was this the enemy who had robbed me of my rest, and almost broken my heart, but the day before? In a few seconds I found myself before a cheerful fire, and had the gratification of seeing the caricature burnt, and of enjoying one of the most sumptuous meals of which I had partaken. Tea being nearly over, my host began:

"You are an artist," said he.

I could not but betray my gratification at his assurance, but wondered how he became possessed of information of my endeavours in that direction. He noticed my astonishment.

"You seem surprised," he continued. "You may not employ pencil and paper, may not be familiar with the smell of paint, but you are nevertheless an artist in soul."

No wonder if I began to be of my host's opinion; still I felt puzzled, and no doubt looked so.

"You," proceeded my new-found friend, "have more of the real artist in you than the whole population of this ancient city put together, and I do not except the archdeacon himself, with all his fine pictures notwithstanding."

"Not excepting the archdeacon himself!" I inwardly exclaimed. "Why, the archdeacon is considered one of the greatest living men." I was lost in bewilderment.

"You shall become my pupil; I have decided that point," said my host, unheeding my silence. "When will you begin?"

All this time the kindly-natured artist had been the only speaker. I had answered with my eyes, and the conversation had been sustained by their assistance. It now, however, became necessary for me to speak, and I answered, that "of all things, I most desired to become an artist" (he seemed gratified at this confirmation of his impressions), "but that I was poor, struggling for bread, up early and late, and therefore I could not become an artist."

"We shall see," was the friendly and encouraging reply. "Can you not find time to take a daily lesson? You can come to my studio between school hours, and of an evening. What say you? Will you come?"

I explained that "my school hours commenced at seven in the morning, that the intervals usually allotted to meals were in my case taken up by the occupation of an errand boy, that I took my food chiefly in the streets, and that the only real leisure I had possessed for a long time past had been spent at his window, as he had seen me; that if I gave up my situation, I should starve, and there was no help for it."

"We shall see," he again observed, in his kindly manner. "Tell me, what is your salary?"

"One shilling and sixpence a week, and some very small trifles besides, but not many."

"It is settled," said the artist. "I will pay you two shillings a week. Become my pupil, you will do me honour, and may be you will one day repay me when I am old and poor. I am not rich now: far from it; but I can do this. So we will consider the matter settled."

CHAPTER XXVII.

PAPER AND PENCILS.

It was Saturday when the artist burnt the caricature. When we parted, he told me to come on the following morning, as he wished to have more talk with me. I was at his house as the clock struck the hour he had named. The artist's breakfast was in readiness. I noticed many things which I had not observed the previous evening, for I had more leisure and more light. He was dressing in the adjoining room, but called out to me to take a seat by the fire. My eyes were never more active, nor more pleasantly occupied. The walls were covered with pictures, and the table with eatables, and both had a fascination for me, for, in addition to my love of art, I had a sound appetite. A pot of coffee and a dish of ham stood before the fire. Everything was calculated to make me feel happy. The streets without were sunny, cold, and still, for the morning bells were hushed, and everybody was at home. I had breakfasted hours before, on those eternal two slices of bread and basin of discoloured hot water, which my aunt called tea, a sort of third mash from twice brewed tea leaves, bought from college servants. The artist's table was laid for two. I was not invited, but this I found Monsieur Dalby (such was his name) assumed, for immediately he made his appearance, rubbing his hands, he, without the smallest ceremony, placed a chair opposite to his own for me, and proceeded to help me to a bountiful portion of the breakfast. All this kindness was near being too much for me. I was well nigh overpowered. Misfortunes out of number had been mine, but no very large amount of kindness had fallen to me. My heart throbbed for the first time; my eyes dilated as if they would burst; I felt a strange twitching in my under lip, sensation new to me then, as my friend kept talking, passing from subject to subject, speaking now of pictures, of the fields, of the woods, returning now and then at intervals to myself, and my prospects, and what he would do for me. I remember every word that he uttered, how every word was kind, and laid in my heart the beginning of that faith in goodness, which has never since left me.

Breakfast ended, the artist busied himself with some drawers and slides in a large cupboard. It was no business of mine to watch his movements. I had somewhere picked up good manners; and I occupied myself with the fire, the mantelpiece, and the ornaments. There was much rustling of paper, and opening and shutting of drawers. At length the artist called me by a Christian name I had never heard myself called by before. I answered to it readily; he looked surprised.

"Robert is not your name?" he said.

"No, sir."

"Then why did you so readily answer to it?"

"I thought you meant it for me."

"I did. I wish to call you by that name. It is an odd fancy, which I would not explain."

My silence expressed all I wished to say, and my interrogator was more than satisfied, as I could see by his looks.

"See here," he called, "is a large roll of paper, which has been stowed away for years, and is getting discoloured. It will be useful to you;" saying which, he put the paper into my arms.

"And here too are many pencils." I thought his voice faltered as he said this. "Take them," said he, "and put them into your pocket: leave not one: and here is a knife, and india-rubber and chalks. Take all, every scrap. And in a hurried, nervous manner, he proceeded to load me, filling my pockets and arms. I grew bewildered, and my emotions this time found relief in tears, which washed away the last dregs of the vagabond.

When I got home I perceived that many of the articles given me were marked in a boyish hand with the name of Robert Dalby, and then I understood all about the name he had called me, and which, as it seemed his pleasure to use it, I accepted, until in process of time and affection it came to supersede my own.

My friendship with M. Dalby commenced in a manner so novel and so happy, continued for little more than a year, as, in order to benefit his fortune, he accepted the post of designer in a porcelain manufactory in another part of the country. At parting, he was kind enough to say that he left the city which loved him not, where he had prospered so little, proud at having found one sincere lover of art in myself, humble as were my pretensions.

I may add, that he left me very little richer than he found me, except in the results of that valued instruction and priceless and unexpected kindness I had received at his hands. I may as well own that I was richer also in ambition, and in possession of a folio, filled with my own productions, which no one would buy, for they were at the best but poor copies of those drawings, which in the first instance had attracted me to M. Dalby's window, and which had possessed so many charms for me. It is not much wonder that they possessed few attractions for the inhabitants. In those days the universities vied with each other in striving which could in the shortest space of time starve any artist who ventured to set up within their walls.

CHAPTER XXVIII.

THE SCHOOL COUNCIL.

I HAD now entered upon my fourteenth year, and become entitled to my dismissal from the Browncoat Boys' Charity School, and to a premium of seven pounds, the sum usually devoted to apprenticing out-going boys. The choice of a master was no easy matter to me. The artistic education I had received did not lessen the difficulty. The school council barely listened to my petition that I might be made a painter of pictures. The rule was to find trades, not professions, for the boys, and I, in common with five or six others, were ordered to find masters who would take us for the money awarded. I prayed them to let me follow the arts, and produced my folio of sketches in support of my pretensions. I call to mind how our treasurer, a portly, wealthy coal merchant, who had risen from nothing (as he told us ten thousand times), looked down upon me from his slightly raised seat. My application appeared to him so extraordinary, that he involuntarily dropped the well-known volume, entitled "The Whole Duty of Man" (the book given to lads on leaving school) and stared me right full in the face: while a rich brewer, also one of the quorum, no less astonished, followed the treasurer's example, and the following interrogatory commenced.

BREWER: "Has the boy any friends?"

MASTER: "I am not aware that he has. Have you any friends, boy?"

BOY: "No, sir."

MASTER: "You have an aunt somewhere?"

BOY: "Yes, sir."

MASTER: "Is she well to do?"

BOY: "She has not a shilling in the world."

MASTER: "Just so."

BREWER (again addressing the master): "Have we any precedent of a boy of this stamp on the books of the school?"

MASTER: "I am happy to say we have not."

COAL MERCHANT: "Your remark is well timed. This boy appears to have altogether mistaken the humble position in life into which it has pleased God to call him. When does he leave school?"

MASTER: "To-day."

BREWER: "Then I fear that we shall not find time to convince him of his error."

MASTER (suggestively): "A sound flogging might still be of service. I have always found the birch very effective in cases of this dogged description."

A master tailor in a small way of business here took part in the conversation. He was apparently amused with the turn matters had taken.

MASTER TAILOR: "Has the boy troubled you much in that way?"

MASTER: "As a rule, he has not been flogged more than three or four times in six days."

MASTER TAILOR: "What have been his offences?"

MASTER: "Keeping bad time, for the most part."

MASTER TAILOR (looking towards me): "Ah, how was it you managed to keep such bad time, boy?"

BOY: "I have had to run of errands between school hours, sir."

COAL MERCHANT: "Why did you run of errands, boy?"

BOY: "Because I could not help it, sir."

COAL MERCHANT: "Because you could not help it, eh! How was that?"

BOY: "I ran of errands first of all, sir, because aunt kept her bed with rheumatism."

COAL MERCHANT: "I don't see what rheumatism has to do with running of errands."

BOY: "Please, sir, I had nothing to eat."

COAL MERCHANT: "Oh, I see, you ran of errands to get something to eat. When did you eat it? when you had got it?"

BOY: "I ate as I could, sir, and sometimes I did not eat at all, sir."

COAL MERCHANT: "That was very remarkable conduct."

MASTER (addressing me): "Don't prevaricate. When did you make those sketches?"

BOY: "I did some at night, and on half holidays. The last year I did not run of errands, because the gentleman paid me to stop at home to draw."

COAL MERCHANT: "And who is this gentleman you speak of?"

BOY: "Mr. Dalby, in Zigzag Lane, sir."

BREWER (addressing the master): "Do you know anything of this Dalby?"

MASTER: "He is a mad-brained fellow, driven here by the revolution, a republican and an infidel to boot. He found no encouragement here, and in consequence recently disappeared from the town, and I rather think not a little in debt."

I need scarcely say that the worthy master was drawing upon his imagination for these disparaging facts, which he supposed to be descriptive of every foreigner.

BREWER: "In debt, eh! Are you in debt, boy?"

BOY: "No, sir."

Brewer: "Are you an infidel?"

Boy: "No, sir."

Brewer: "Did you ever draw on Sunday?"

Boy: "Yes, sir."

Brewer: "And why did you do that?"

Boy: "I couldn't help it, sir."

Brewer: "How not, help it? What do you mean by that?"

Boy: "I was so very fond of drawing, sir."

Brewer: "Did you not know that it was wicked to draw on the Sabbath?"

Boy: "Yes, sir."

Brewer: "Then why did you do it?"

Boy: "I did not draw on Sundays at first."

Brewer: "What did you do at first, then?"

Boy: "I only cut my pencils and looked at my drawings at first—and then I drew a little."

Brewer: "And then a good deal?"

Boy: "Yes, sir."

Brewer: "And then, by little and little, you have gone on and on, until you have arrived at the condition in which you are?"

At this point the coal merchant looked at his watch, and reminded the brewer that it was dinner time, whereupon that gentleman ceased his labours of interrogation and concluded by remarking that I "should prove of little credit to the institution, or of service to myself, or anybody else." "There is no knowing," said the coal merchant; "for, as I have often remarked, I came from nothing myself."

With this qualified prediction of the man who had "risen from nothing" I was relieved from my disagreeable position, received the customary volume entitled the "Whole Duty of Man," and went forth into the town to look for a master. My aunt could not sleep a wink for the responsibility which thus devolved upon her. She consulted her neighbours, and the report that "a lad of promise" (so went the description) being in want of a master spread over the parish: and among the first a popular barber beckoned me into his hair-cutting rooms, and offered me the opportunity of assisting him in clipping the hair of urchins and shaving grooms and carters. He assured me that he would make a man of me and put me in a fair way of making my fortune. He said he had long been in want of a youth who could sketch. No profession, he insisted, stood more in need of an artistic capacity than his. There was plain work, it was true, which did not require extraordinary talent; but in the higher branches of the business a good eye, skilful handling, and cultivated taste were indispensable, as I should discover. I declined the hairdresser's offer with many thanks: and something which I said elicited a laugh from a half-starved parish apprentice who seemed never to have laughed before; and while the barber was pulling his ears, I walked out of the shop.

A poor, tottering, tallow-faced tailor also fancied that the "bit of money," the seven pounds, might be useful to him, as no doubt it would, if appearances were to be trusted. He had come to make my acquaintance from having made my clothes. He had ventured on a contract to manufacture the heavy, tough, leather breeches worn by the Brown Coat Boys, and had made his estimate by far too modest. The material moreover had proved new to him, and had cost him many a sigh. Before the seventy and odd garments were completed he had broken his shears and undermined his constitution most woefully. He was candid enough to tell my aunt all this, and to add that he had never thought to be able to endure the sight of a Brown Coat Boy again, so long as he lived; but that, taking all things into account, seeing that he was well nigh past working for himself, and he already owned a number of apprentices, three from the Brown Boys, two from the workhouse, and four of his own sons, making up the cabalistic number nine, he was resolved on attempting the decimal quantity, and undertook to take me, provided I would promise to be very steady and obedient—all of which I civilly declined: and thus ended my opportunities of distinguishing myself as barber or tailor.

CHAPTER XXIX.

THE OLD CARVER.

During my intimacy with M. Dalby I frequently saw an old carver at the studio. He came to consult my instructor on the subject of church restoration. He had been engaged in the toilsome labour of restoring one of the most ancient and interesting churches in the city. Occasionally I had gone to the church with drawings which the carver had commissioned my master to make for the guidance of his staff in their operations on the crumbling walls. The old carver was skilful beyond anything I had seen in my life. He would spend an incredible time in freeing the delicate tracery of the monkish chisel from paint and whitewash, plastered and daubed thereon by modern churchwardens. It was impossible not to perceive how light, how chaste, and crisp, the ancient workmanship came out beneath the fingers of the patient manipulator. But what surprised and pleased me most was to see the carver replace absent portions which time or damp had decayed or barbarians defaced. The stone seemed to grow before my eyes, and the foliage to spread itself out even as I had seen it do on the warm bank in spring time. My eye wandered from the work to the tools, from the tools to the workman. It was all magic to me. There was music in the very click of the steel, that woke up the echoes of the vaulted church, like voices answering one another. With intimacy came confidence, and I would venture now and then to pick up a chisel from among the many that lay upon the planks, where the old man sat, and curiously examine it as I would a thing that had life in it and would do what it was bidden to do.

In my troubles I was suddenly reminded of the old carver. Would he take me as his apprentice and teach me the wonders of his art? The thought relieved my mind from all its doubts and griefs. I went to his house; he was still at his work. I flew to the church. It was night, and only a glimmering candle revealed the whereabouts of the worker. I scaled the ladders and crossed the scaffolding at the risk of my life, in order to learn my fate before I slept. How many a poor boy has been troubled as I was then, seeking, longing for an insight into those mysteries (for art and mystery go hand in hand) which should bring him profit and honour in the future. I approached the old man in his solitude like an apparition, but he started not. He calmly laid aside his chisel, and, taking up the candle, surveyed me from head to foot. In a few words I made known my desire. What better introduction could I have than to be able to call myself the pupil of M. Dalby? He received me with animation. His dream was fulfilled. He would have me, he said, although I brought him not a farthing. I might spend the seven pound in clothes and tools. I should become his right hand. When would I begin? Why not begin then? I had no objection: he lent me tools, and to work I went. Before the clock struck nine I had earned a shilling to buy some supper, and not before I wanted it. It had been an anxious day. I had not eaten for twelve long hours.

CHAPTER XXX.

THE CARVER'S HOME.

WHENEVER it was practicable, which was frequently the case, the old carver and myself worked together. He liked somebody to talk to, who had no wish to interrupt his enthusiastic garrulity; and no one of any taste would desire more, or better, than to listen to the anecdotes of work and workers with which his mind was stored. He had passed his life in churches and cathedrals. He conceived that churches were built and allowed to decay "in order that they might be restored." With him restoration was an art. To model, cast, carve and pick, were all the delights he had. The rubbish of the dark ages, apparently without form or purpose, came out sharp and precise from his touch. He could see through an incrustation as thick as a wall. All the churchwardens of successive generations, with their lime, mortar and paint, had not been able so far to efface the handiwork of the mediæval artist, but that my master could recover it; and so far from blaming the "Goths," he owed them a debt of gratitude for the trouble they had been at to destroy. But for Vandalism, he used to say, he might never have been a restorer. Months passed by, and the chaos of mouldering architecture began to wear marks of intelligent design, and every day and hour the work increased the friendship between the patriarch and his assistant. In the dark winter I have seen the old man numbed with the cold, and have crept stealthily away from his side, and procured from his housekeeper some soup, coffee, or a cup of spiced ale, and then we have sat down together, removed from the chatter, banter, and boasting of the masons and labourers, and enjoyed such happy intervals of rest as only thoughtful and hearty labour yields. If I am asked what I think of those early days of my life, I might be led to say that I could not wish to see them over again, and yet I was often so happy that words could but ill express the serenity that took possession of me. There was in that union of the old and young heart something very strange—a reversal, as it would appear to observers, of the order of nature. In my very boyhood Old Age singled me out, as I have indicated, and, laying its attenuated hand upon my shoulder, exclaimed, "Thou art mine! sit thee down, and let us talk of the past." The respect and affection I entertained for my companion were not of that kind which every well-ordered child instinctively feels for grey hairs. It was long before I could comprehend the meaning of this difference in my case, but my experience has since explained it to me over and over again. The old carver's heart was still young. The heart of the true artist never grows old.

In addition to executing large commissions for the restoration of churches and cathedrals, my friend and master had established a manufactory of *terra cotta* ware, consisting of vases, gods, goddesses, heroes, and philosophers, chiefly after the antique, but some few of them from designs by a contiguous Italian, one Signor Bezza. This Signor Bezza lived with his daughter in a cottage near the workshops, and acted in the capacity of foreman over a number of men, two of whom also were natives of Italy. The various casts in plaster or clay were distributed upon the floor, or in the garden, arranged in seeming negligence, yet in reality for the better effect which they thus produced.

My master's house contained several large rooms, which had been constructed in a somewhat rude fashion out of a spacious barn or granary, the outer shell or original exterior being preserved intact; the uncouth effect of dark beams and bricks being mitigated by a profusion of ivy, which had grown unmolested until it well-nigh choked up the windows. I found, on going to reside in this queer mansion, almost every available portion of space crowded with carvings in wood and stone. The housekeeper, indeed, found great difficulty in putting me up a bed. After much discussion and many experiments, I was accommodated by an encroachment upon the largest lumber room—a grim example of Gothic genius, and a very limbo of worm-eaten decorations. By the aid of a huge, clumsy screen, mortar, and white-wash, we extemporised a very excellent domicile and study, into which we admitted sufficient sunlight by curtailing to some extent the trellis of dark ivy leaves without. In less than a week I felt as settled in my new home as if I had been born and reared in it. For a few nights only my dreams were a little disturbed by the presence of a flickering light and constant rumblings among the carvings. It was an inveterate habit with the old carver to linger among his antiques long after I had gone to rest. The curiosities underwent a sort of nightly classification and labelling. It was the belief of their owner that every morsel contained in the museum would one day "come in," and under that impression the meanest fragment was preserved with miserly care.

In the more dilapidated buildings which received our renovating attentions it sometimes became necessary to consult our crumbling stores for authorities, and they often would have been of great use in clearing up doubts as to the style, shape, and expression of certain griffins and other monsters which had been destroyed by barbarous zealots in olden times, but it somehow usually happened that the right monster was not to be found in its right place in our collection. The collector had a marvellous faculty for confounding his dingy relics. However, one good at least came out of them—they served to make my venerable instructor exceedingly happy and contented, especially at seasons when no great work of restoration was on hand. I had some suspicion that the antiquary classified his faithful pupil with his antiques, for he made it a rule never to go to bed without paying me a stealthy visit, to see whether I was safe, and I wondered that he did not label me with the rest of his treasures.

The window of my studio looked into the pleasant little garden where Signor Bezza cultivated wall-fruit and herbs for salads. My window-sill was formed by an ancient wall or buttress, which in summer was covered by gilly-flowers of the richest fragrance: and when not engaged in modelling, drawing, or carving, I was accustomed to read at this casement, for I had become a student in books, and my studies included not only works bearing directly upon my profession, but extended over a wide range of standard literature, both in prose and in verse. It was seldom that I lay down at night without passing a brief period of meditation at my window. It was here that I summed up the actions of my early days. I was now happy and could look back and smile at the little vicissitudes through which I had passed, and which my faithful memory retained in all their vividness of reality. Often I thought of my first, great, absent friend, who taught me the rudiments of my art,—and of the old man who daily imparted to me something of the experience of his long life, and who cared for me as if I had been his own. It seemed that at this time I had no want.

Three years had passed away, and during all that time I had scarcely been idle for a day. I had grown comparatively wealthy, and had laid up a store of art-treasures for the future. In addition to my library, I possessed many fine prints, which I had selected from the folios of a printseller in the city. Moreover, I had a number of casts from ancient sculptures which the Italian, Signor Bezza, had given me. He had often vainly tried to allure me from the "mediæval barbarisms," as he termed our Gothic, to the glories of Greece and Italy; but I had so long dwelt among quaint examples of the monastic chisel, that I was as averse to the graceful proportions of the Athenian sculptors as the owl is to the light of day. There came a time, notwithstanding, when the Signor, with his Dianas and Apollos, gained the victory over the griffins of the dark ages. Hitherto he had only invited me to the workshop, and while he confined his illustrations of the beautiful to inanimate stone and plaster the conflict between the classic and the Gothic was undecided. One night the sculptor invited me to partake of a dish of salad, prepared after the manner of his own country, in order that we might discuss the great art question at our leisure. The Signorina was present, and, what with the father's arguments and the daughter's grace, the whole subject of the Antique *versus* Gothic appeared in a far more interesting and classic guise. That night the period devoted to meditation at my casement was much longer than ordinary. At parting the Signorina had, with her own hand, presented me with a basket of peaches from her garden, and also a piece of blue silk embroidered with gold, which I chanced to admire, and which she told me had formed part of her holiday dress when a child. In return, I promised to paint her a picture, and to introduce the precious relic of her childhood along with the peaches, after the manner of a certain Dutch master.

CHAPTER XXXI.

THE OLD CARVER'S STORY.

THE morning after my visit to the cottage of Signor Bezza, I found myself in a very unsatisfactory state of mind. My master had, only the previous day, set me to model an eagle, which he had been commissioned to carve in oak, for the reading-desk of one of the churches which we had renovated. With shame I say it, the eloquence and beauty I had found at the table of my new intimates, the Italians, had almost obliterated the eagle from my memory. My sketch, which had been approved, lay neglected on the bench, while the clay for the model lay covered up with damp cloths, untouched. The old man, as was his wont, came to call me to an early breakfast. "Earn your breakfast before you eat it," was one of his wholesome, old-fashioned maxims. I had not earned my breakfast on this morning, and made no scruple of informing my master of the fact.

"Not earned your breakfast?" he asked in the kindest manner.

I pointed to the uncovered clay.

"You are unwell."

"I was never better."

"What, then, am I to understand?" he half wonderingly observed.

I directed his attention to a group of still-life, consisting of the fragment of an antique vase, around which I had arranged, in graceful folds, the blue embroidered silk which the Signorina had given me, so as to relieve most forcibly the peaches which I had placed in front on a slab of rich Sienna marble: the whole presenting a choice of forms and a variety of harmonious tints which would have charmed the heart of that famous painter, Van Aelst.

The carver fixed his eyes for a few moments on the group, and then asked what it meant.

"If," said he, "you have grouped these objects merely for contemplation, I shall offer no objection to your harmless whim, whatever I might feel respecting a medley of Flemish, Grecian and Italian productions: but, if you have set your mind on painting these things, may I ask from whom you have received the commission? I trust it is all a momentary freak of fancy."

"Sir," I answered, with the frankness he had taught me to observe, "this is no freak of fancy, but a matter upon which I have set my heart. I will rise early, I will work late,—the eagle shall be my masterpiece, but only say that I may paint my beautiful composition."

"And when it is finished, and when you have outrivalled the Dutchman, what purpose will it answer?"

"It will enable me to keep a promise I have made, and which is of such a nature that I cannot break it. It is but twelve hours since I last saw you at St. Margaret's Church, and then I had not a thought of this undertaking, nor had I care or sorrow, or doubt or misgiving on any one thing."

"Tell me no more. I have foreseen this hour and dreaded it; my daily vigilance have not preserved thee from the blandishments of Signor Bezza. You are in love with his daughter, and—but I cannot blame you." Here the old man passed his hand over his brow, as though the thought gave him anguish.

"Sir," I exclaimed, "do not misjudge me. I am your pupil still—will do all that you ask of me."

"I know it;" sighed the old man, "I believe that you are true to me; and that you will continue faithful to me when you have heard the story of my troubles, I do not doubt."

After breakfast, which passed without further remark, the old man began a narrative to which it was impossible to me to listen without surprise and emotion.

"I am old enough," said he, "to remember the time when in this country native talent, and all that was venerable and national, were sacrificed to a false taste for what was denominated the "classical," but which in fact was nothing more than a hollow mockery and a pretence. For a time the solemn architecture of England, the forms and patterns of her religious temples and ancestral halls, were set aside for feeble imitations of Greek and Roman types. Noblemen and country squires built their park lodges after Athenian models, and their summer-houses after Roman villas. They raised altars where no sacrifices were intended; they had shrines without priests, and gods and goddesses without religion. People gave themselves classic airs and graces. Ladies of rank were painted or sculptured in the characters of Diana and Venus, and Silvia and Delia. Obese aldermen fancied themselves Roman senators, and members of parliament persuaded themselves that they bore a strong resemblance to the Demostheneses and Ciceros of antiquity. Every statue put up in honour of the dead or the living appeared in the garb of some illustrious consul or emperor of the classic world. Poetry and painting followed in the current. Amorous bards, who had slumbered for ages unheeded, were exhumed as it were from the grave, and scholars and famed versifiers turned the Latin of Ovid and Sappho into the language of Shakespeare. I came when this artificial art, as I will term it, had reached its culminating point, and rescued the Gothic chisel from the rust. I found discerning patrons who could distinguish betwixt the true interests of art and the vapid and fulsome plagiarisms which had so long prevailed. The reaction was, as I persuaded myself, complete. It became my task not so much to create as to rescue the sacred relics of our forefathers from the obscurity to which neglect and disrespect had consigned them. Thus have I spent my days among the blackened beams and rafters, where the owl and the bat made their homes in the carved and emblazoned roof. I found quaintly tesselated pavements immured beneath wooden planks, and slender columns of precious marble buried beneath whitewash and plaster. With knowledge and energy, in patience and endurance, I pursued my course, often unrequited, to rescue those rare monuments of the past; for next to the creative artist I esteem the worker whose labour tends to restore lost traces of power and originality in the works of the great dead. The mock classic rage declined, as I thought, for good. I was deceived. Like the returning tide of the sea, the false classics returned to cover the land with stucco, plaster and terra cotta. Again the park-gates and mansions of the nobility were made to caricature the ancients, and gardens and lawns to mimic their solemn groves. Again the antique appeared in every variety of material, and adapted to unheard-of purposes. Architects, sculptors, glass-blowers, potters, brass-founders, and furniture-makers fell in with the revived order of things, and squares, streets, town-halls, session-houses, city churches, and even jails and village chapels were constructed after the antique. Again the Gothic sank into its former state of neglect. It grieved me sore to part with my old hands. Where I had work for a score of able carvers, I found hardly sufficient for myself.

"It was at this turn in my affairs, when almost disheartened, when I had no longer youth on my side, that this Signor Bezza came here bragging of his Cellini-like powers. I will not tell you of half of what he could do—it would be far easier to enumerate the few accomplishments of which he was *not* master. He would, he said, furbish up our crumbling old city for us. He would, with a few strokes of his wand, transform our ruined walls into a second Athens. He would remould us and give us new faces. He would so embellish us that we should not know where we were. He described our city as more resembling the churchyard of ancient kings whose very names were lost in the remote past than the abode of the living. We were everything that was dingy; we were the rubbish of barbarism itself. Our spacious English halls, of English oak, he designated barns and stables; our cathedrals were dungeons: and our churches malt-houses. He said all this and more. I have given you a sample of his off-hand pretentious style of talking. He had a smoother and modester tone for the gentry. He worked his way: he exhibited works of art as his own which were the fruit of other men's genius. He got pity, admiration, and encouragement from some of our best men. He was brought to me all smiles. He was described as a man without money, but abounding in talent which might be turned to account. Of all men in the world, my friend the Archdeacon St. John himself stood his advocate, and implored me to take up with the new stucco-and-plaster madness. 'It will bring in money,' said the Archdeacon. 'You want a fortune for your boy.' My boy was just leaving school. 'You want a fortune for your boy.' I had not thought of that. For the first time I lost some little of my faith in the Gothic chisel: and my poor boy, the image of his mother, looked up, as it were from the tomb, in support of the project. 'What would you have me do, Archdeacon?' I asked. 'The matter is very simple;' he replied, 'conform to the times, which will not conform to you.' 'True, Mr. Archdeacon,' observed Signor Bezza, 'the matter is very simple.

What can be more so? Give me a shed, a few loads of sand and clay, and permit me,' he said (addressing me), 'to build you a simple kiln, and I will make you wealthy, provide a fortune for your child, and not once interfere with your taste for native architecture; you will as you please continue your invaluable restorations.' 'Well; the Archdeacon, God forgive him, succeeded on behalf of his Italian friend. Signor Bezza came, and, to do him justice, he laboured like a slave. At first bread and water would serve him and his companions (those two Italians who even now form part of his staff). The kiln was built, the sand and clay procured, the models made or imported from town. It was all very wonderful to see. No Englishman could have done it in so short a time, and for so small a sum of money. My son entered his department, and showed talent; and when I saw my boy in, as I thought, a fair way of business, I will own, I felt less prejudiced, and parted with my savings with less reluctance; in fact, I spent every available pound upon the new scheme. I can say that from the first hour of our acquaintance the Signor had not given me an uncivil word. If I rebuked him, he would express his obligation to me. If I resented any act of his, he would bow his head; and yet he is not mild by nature, but wrathful in the extreme. Deceived by his fair speech (and I believe that he equally deceived himself), one fatal day I made him a partner in the terra-cotta department. Henceforth he became my master. He took to my boy, and flattered me. The Signorina was then a child, a beautiful child. I see them now, growing up together like brother and sister, the olive and the rose entwined, as the Signor said (my boy was fair, and the Signorina dark). But where now is my boy? Victim to the most enthralling and ruinous of all vices—gambling. This Bezza, under the pretence of giving harmless salad suppers (after the fashion of his country) invited other adventurers, reckless like himself, turning night into day. Of course the terra-cotta trade failed, and my boy, my once dutiful boy, soon half beggared me by his follies and extravagances. But I will bring my story to a close. The boy lies by his mother's side, where his father will soon follow him."

CHAPTER XXXII.

THE SIGNORINA'S PICTURE.

THAT Signor Bezza had not acted honestly by my master was certain. Something might be attributed to prejudice on the part of the Gothic carver. The savings of fifty years of anxious toil had been dissipated, and the old man rendered almost dependent upon the labour of his hands in extreme old age. From myself, his apprentice, he had, he would kindly own, received all the attention and affection of a son. On reflection, he did not desire me to neglect the picture, which he found me desirous of painting. On the contrary, he urged forward the work, and gave me leisure, in order that it might be perfected before the peaches had lost their bloom. He even went so far as to promise a costly frame when the work was complete, and confessed to me, that he would render his assistance with pleasure, for that he loved the Signorina as the early playmate of his lost boy. The peaches being the most perishable objects of my composition, I had prudently completed them first, reserving the drapery, vase, and marble slab.

Since I had parted from M. Dalby I had never ceased in my leisure hours from cultivating my taste for the art of painting. I had found the more facility in pursuing my evening studies, owing to that gentleman having left for my use nearly the whole of the furniture of his studio. Thus provided with abundance of materials, I had made a practice of selecting for study such objects in nature as the garden furnished; either of fruit, plants, or flowers; sometimes bringing in the distant prospect, as seen from my window. In carrying out our restorations, we more than once obtained access to famous picture galleries, and, among many other works of the old schools, I had been particularly struck with two pictures by Van Aelst, a famous painter of flowers, fruit, insects, shells, and costly plate. As a carver and modeller, I had acquired much instruction from the contemplation of this artist's productions. His execution, to my mind, seemed miraculous. One of the two pictures in question, to which I gave the preference, was very simple in its arrangement; three fresh, ripe peaches, with a few leaves attached, lay upon a silver salver, beside a Venetian goblet of the purest mould, and apparently as fragile as a soap bubble, so that, looking at it, one fancied that a gust of wind might dissipate it into air. This goblet formed a mirror, in which was vividly portrayed an almost interminable Dutch street, with its quays, canals, and shipping, just as it would appear through a lattice. A heap of grapes, well set off by a few sharp, variegated leaves, a table-cover of olive-green velvet, and some insects, completed the group. While I do not regard extreme finish as the highest excellence in carved work, still I must admit that a delicate manipulation and high finish have ever appeared great charms in my eyes. When the artist first surveys the shapeless block of wood given him for the purpose of realising some set form, it is no easy matter to reduce the cumbrous mass into a working state. The process called "bosteing" is very difficult. Unless the worker has a good eye, he runs the risk of cutting away too much wood in some parts, and of leaving a superabundance in others, especially where he works without a model; and even where the model is present, the mechanical appliances used by wood-carvers are commonly confined to ordinary callipers, so that a good eye for proportion is still indispensable. As far, then, as the mere roughing-in of the work goes, I know that little assistance can be obtained from any external source. The wood-carver at least must possess great capacity, and have had extensive practice, to ender him expert in all that relates to the preliminary portions of his work. But when the risk and difficulties of the preliminary stages are past, then the advantages of consulting the elaborate examples of the Dutch masters become evident. In all that relates to texture and high finish, the sharp, crisp, and sparkling touch of a Van Aelst, Huysum, or De Heem, will be apt to prompt the carver to the exercise of his highest powers. It was by first consulting Van Aelst's pictures of still-life, to assist me in some carvings on which I was engaged, that my eye became enamoured of their rich and glowing tints, and I was led irresistibly in trifles, to try my pencil in that direction.

The Signorina's flattering present revived the desire already lurking in my breast, of producing a masterpiece in imitation of the Dutchman. But as it turned out, I was never well pleased with my performance. I had resolved that on its completion I would direct all my energies to my old master's interests. The charm, therefore, which might otherwise have animated my pencil had departed with the first hour of the work. The folds of azure blue and golden embroidery on the silk had lost their grace; the antique vase, the polished marble, and radiant fruit, looked heavy and tasteless. Decay, too, set in, and one morning, on looking for the peaches, I found them rotten, as if to foretell the death of my hopes. I had learned that the Signorina already had a lover. I had seen her during the progress of the picture, and words had fallen from her lips which pained me, because I could but regard them as the language of mere friendship. It grieved her, she would say, that I should on her account sit immured in my solitary room. It was the time of gipsy parties, and she sent to give me intimation of one of those pleasant excursions. She and her friends would be there. At the last moment she came to my window in the garden. I caught sight of her, and, judging from her manner that she wished to speak to me, I went out. She had come to implore me to lay aside my work. She would make me promise to join her party, and gave me exact instructions where they would encamp; I could bring paper and pencil and sketch. What could be more pleasant? It was wrong to refuse her. I was looking ill. She would be herself unhappy if she saw me not at the party. I promised her that I would follow her advice, said that I knew the chosen spot where they had arranged to assemble: it was one of my favourite haunts. She might expect me; and I thanked her many times for her solicitude.

While we were thus speaking, she was looking for a flower; and having fixed upon a china rose, which grew up near my window, I hastened to my studio to pluck it. I shall not attempt to describe how lovely she looked as she cast up her eyes after the flower. She wore a simple straw hat; her tiny hand had been compressed into a minute kid glove, of a pale lemon tint; while her hair, black as the raven's, hung down in sportive tresses. Having given her the rose she desired, she was so pleased with it that she gave me further pleasure by asking me for its companion. At the risk of breaking my neck, I plucked the second one pointed out, and then with a laugh and a bound she tripped lightly away. In a few seconds I saw her enter her father's cottage. All the time she had been talking to me another had been waiting for her at the end of the avenue, and the companion rose was for him.

CHAPTER XXXIII.

THE GIPSY PARTY.

WHEN, as a boy, compelled to work myself, I saw those of my own years in the playground happy and boisterous, I felt no envy. When later in life, labouring in the studio of M. Dalby, I saw through the window troops of youths going forth into the fields, with bat, ball, and kite, so far from feeling disappointed, that I could not join in their health-giving pastimes,—so far from feeling discontented with my lot,—the smile of satisfaction which lit up the faces of the juvenile throng imparted real joy to my heart. I loved the streets most when they were most silent, when the boisterous element was far away: but I also liked to be conscious that the multitude were bent on happiness. On such holiday occasions I have pointed my crayon with a relish, and set down to my design in a state of mind such as the tired usher feels when the school is closed, and he has before him a few hours he can really and truly call his own. I tried to revive the old state of blissful serenity when I beheld the joyous Signorina depart for the woods with her equally joyous lover, wearing on their breasts the roses I had plucked from the window of my studio. I gathered all my implements about me, displayed my choicest prints upon the screen, brought out my antique, reached forth my favourite volume. All the old conditions surrounded me, but their enchantment was gone. The Signorina alone remained mistress of my thoughts. Within all was gloomy as the night; but when I cast my eyes over the landscape a track of sunlight marked the way which the lovers had taken through the meadows and up the hill side.

The poet tells us how the Indian lover rose unconsciously from his sleep, and how "a spirit in his feet" led him, "he knew not how," unto the window of his mistress. In some such dreamy state of inspired unconsciousness I found myself in the fields, in search of the Italian maiden. A rapid walk brought me in sight of the gipsy encampment, where I paused; passion had carried me thus far, but principle now arrested my steps. I had forsaken a friendless old man, who had befriended me, for one who, possessing youth, beauty and accomplishments, might command any number of friends and admirers. Besides, was it not clear as the day that the heart I sought was no longer free? Wherefore then my headlong course? I turned down a quiet lane to reflect, and whence I might easily retrace my steps. Merry shouts and peals of laughter, came over the meadows. It was a bright day, and many wild flowers still lingered on the warm embankment. The bee, too, was there, busily gathering in her winter stores. Immovable, I sat watching the tiny insects running to and fro in the grass. A nest of ants lay at my feet, I became interested in their labours, and by degrees the cloud that obscured the summit of my hopes was dispelled, and I could once more think upon the future without despair. I had achieved a position already, and I could yet command respect. Nothing would be denied me, if I could but take a lesson from the minute labourers, the ants at my feet. I would seek in work the solace of disappointed hopes; I had passed through the fire of experience, not unscathed it might be, but I had only to labour with a purpose. Had I not read how the great artists of old found in work a solace for every ill? Was I not fortunate, indeed, thus to be placed in the very pathway to fortune and distinction? An outcast, a wanderer, I might yet come to hold communion with the immortal few. Soliloquizing in this strain, I rose from the ground, and turned, silent and lonely, my way towards home, confident that henceforth I could look on the Signorina with the eye of a Stoic.

The evening was closing in apace. It had been one of those autumn days when sudden storms arise. Suddenly I became conscious of the absence of light in the distant valley and on the woods. Clouds obscured the sun, and I guessed by these appearances that the gay party upon the hill side would take alarm, and soon be upon my track. I was not wrong. The next moment the hum of many voices announced their approach. I stepped hastily aside. The company drew nearer, the lovers among the rest, I cast one look on the Signorina as she passed. On that instant a sunbeam burst through the trees, and fell upon the group: and the same ray which lit up the face of the Italian girl, as in the pride of youth and beauty she leaned on the arm of her lover, also threw the shadow of a stooping, decrepid old man upon an embankment of white loam near where I stood. It was the shadow of the old carver. He had wandered forth in search of his only friend, and found him true. Principle had triumphed over Passion.

CHAPTER XXXIV.

THE OLD CARVER'S LAST WORK.

DAY by day the venerable carver stood more and more in need of those attentions due from youth to old age, but which—alas! for human nature—youth too often fails to render. Never was a more beautiful thought chiselled in stone than the group by Canova, of "Beneficence leading an Old Man to the Tomb." Stricken with years, the patriarch leans on the arms of a young girl, in whose face patience, tenderness, and solicitude are strongly impressed. She walks slowly and softly, as if to accommodate the tottering movements of her decrepid charge, while her eyes are bent upon the ground, as if to choose the smoothest pathway. The mute eloquence of this simple allegory goes direct to the heart; and who does not confess the force of that appeal, indicating so gracefully, and yet so touchingly, the duties of the young and buoyant to the infirm and old? Among others, a cast of this work of Canova's stood in our garden, having been originally purchased by Bezza for casting. I know not that I needed the instant presence of example to direct me in my duty to the old carver; but I was nevertheless grateful to the sculptor for his beautiful and impressive lesson.

Of late my master had devoted himself almost wholly to the completion of a monumental design in remembrance of his wife and child. He had made a great secret of this work; it was not until warned of his near end, that he communicated even to myself his intention of at once placing his last great effort in the chancel of St. Margaret's Church. He had so arranged it that only his own name would be required to make the design complete, and this trifling but delicate task he confided to his pupil. "When I am gone," said he, in an unfaltering voice, "go, unseen, into the Church of St. Margaret, and, with the same chisel I myself employed, cut deeply my name upon the vacant space which I have left on my monument to receive it."

The memorial itself was worthy of the greatest of sculptors—it was unique alike in conception and execution. While it displayed the characteristic tendency of its designer's mind, after the finer and more elaborate examples of the mediæval times, it also placed beyond a doubt the fact that he was no slave to the mannerisms of the dark age. He had gone direct to nature for the materials—the heart alone inspired the idea. In an attitude of mourning, his long lean hands half buried in his dishevelled locks, sat the figure of the bereaved sculptor, in his ordinary working dress—while by his side were strewed the mallet, chisel, and other tools which had been used in engraving the names of mother and child upon an upright slab. The charm of the design rested chiefly in the mound or grave, on which in an apparently natural order the artist had sculptured almost every wild flower to be found in meadow and lane. It was just as if village children had gone forth and plucked whole lapfuls of daffodils, blue bells, cowslips and primroses, and, having thrown them upon the grave, a miracle had turned them into marble. Thus had the sculptor, regardless of toil, lingered over the shrine of his affections—year after year exhausting spring, summer, and autumn of their beauties, from the first snowdrop even to the last dry leaf. The slenderest stalk, the smallest flower, and the tiniest blade of grass were rendered with the extremest finish. Here and there, just as if the winds had so arranged it, were little clefts and hollows formed by dry, mossgrown sticks, so as to impart a lightness to the overhanging flowers: and ever and anon the eye of the observer might detect some more fragile bud and blossom protected beneath the shadow of the huge burdock. And yet with all this variety and profusion there was little appearance of labour or care. The whole seemed like the creation of an hour. It had been the task of many happy intervals, extending over a period of ten years. The dying artist was very proud of this monument, and grew very anxious to see it in its place. There was little difficulty in the way. A fine light space in the side aisle was at once accorded to it, and in a few days, and almost unseen by one of the parishioners, the cherished tribute of genius and affection was securely imbedded in its place. From that hour the ancient carver never more touched mallet or chisel. It seemed a great relief to him that his memorial was at last in its place. He became more cheerful, but, as if for very lack of using them, his eyes grew dim, and by and by he lost his sight altogether. Notwithstanding, his heart and hopes remained fresh and sound as of yore, and he still continued to dilate on the wonderful restorations he had made, and of the great conflicts he had sustained against the false classicists.

It was his fancy to stand or sit in the sun, leaning against the hollow trunk of a leafless, pollard oak, that stood in the hedgerow of the garden. While I was busy in the studio, he would go noiselessly out of the house, and grope his way to his favourite haunt, and there, leaning upon his staff, he would seem to gaze up towards the sun, and intently listen to the larks which rose up from the neighbouring fields.

At length he took to his chamber; but, whether in his garden or his room, he talked of nothing save his restorations, and of his indefatigable efforts to stave off inundations of stucco and plaster. His wants were very few, for in his last days he only asked for water and sunlight. I made sad havoc with the ivy, in order to let the sunbeams into his room. At last he grew deaf, and could no longer derive pleasure from the music of the larks. This of course only led him to talk the more: and totally and happily oblivious of the sad confusion into which his pecuniary affairs had fallen, he would tell me how that I was to consider his stock-in-trade, his mallets, chisels, drawings, models, and fragments of wood and stone carvings, all as my own—for that I was indeed his son. I thanked him over and over again, although I knew that certain creditors were waiting, wolf-like, at the door, to sweep off the entire establishment the moment the poor old man was conveyed to his last home. One morning, to my own great grief and to the satisfaction of the said creditors, we carried the old man, by the little porch, towards the churchyard. The door of the little porch was closed by strangers' hands. I never afterwards saw the interior of the quaint old dwelling. I understood that the relics sold for a trifle, and in a few months a fine villa residence occupied the site of the old carver's cottage.

Thus lived and died the last of the old school of

carvers. He was one of the few whose integrity manifested itself in small things as well as great. I have known him decline a commission rather than employ a material in the smallest way unfitted for the purpose in view. For instance, if the timber at his command had not been tested by the weather for a specified number of seasons, no persuasion would induce him to use it. He would wait until the proper wood, or stone, as the case might be, could be procured: so that, what with the period consumed in taking precautionary measures and the time devoted to imparting the most scrupulous finish to everything, it was no wonder that the rising generation grew impatient, and took up with new modes more in keeping with the impetuous and shallow character of the new age. It but ill suited the temper of your moderns to wait the old carver's time.

CHAPTER XXXV.

THE GARDENER AND HIS PRINTS.

After I had quietly settled down with the old carver in the museum of antiquities, my aunt as quietly betook herself off to her native village, quite satisfied with the part she had played towards myself, and equally convinced that another winter spent in the vegetable market, exposed to all weathers, would be the death of her. On the breaking up of the carver's establishment, therefore, I, in common with the rest of his staff, had to find a new home.

Among our few intimates was a gardener, a sort of half woodman, who lived in a cottage in the suburbs, and got a livelihood chiefly by attending to some shrubberies, walks, and plantations, without the city, belonging to one of the university foundations. He was a man of some taste in his calling; and of this taste my master had for many years availed himself. Few gardens were arranged with nicer feeling and effect than the old carver's. The gardener's family were all grown up and married off, so that he was able to spare me two rooms in his cottage, and for the same reason the dame, his partner, found leisure to dress my meals and wait upon me. The cottage, like its occupants, was of a very plain description. Yet it was pleasant at least in summer, for the tenant had enclosed it with a double row of willow stakes, which as designed had taken root, and, being constantly trimmed, had become a wall of fresh leaves. Within the little front enclosure the owner cultivated flowers, at the rear of the cottage grew vegetables for home use. Here for a time I lived in quiet, mourning my loss, and wondering, half bewildered, what I should do. I had fallen in with the carver's habits so effectually that, like him, I had become almost helpless to battle with the world. My early experience hardly served me. In fact I had become an art student, with a slender purse and no lack of cares. I had shared the fortunes of a poor man. My wealth lay chiefly in my youth and skill. I was, however, enabled to fit up my sitting room as a studio. I had panels, colours, brushes, an easel, engravings and books, together with a great number of tools used in wood and stone carving. All these I arranged in my room in proper order and sat down to reflect. Much solitude had made me reflective. For several days I did nothing else.

My landlord, who had imbibed some little of my old master's love for curiosities, had in the course of years picked up at sales and elsewhere some queer specimens of furniture, china, and a few engravings. Among the prints were two after Gainsborough. One representing cows and horses assembled in a group on the border of a wood, with a rustic fellow lying asleep with his face half buried in the grass. The other was from the celebrated painting by the same master, of a country girl with a pitcher. I had long envied the gardener the possession of these two prints. They were very fine impressions; I was not alone in my desire to possess them. A near neighbour, a money-lender, well known to the undergraduates of the university, had also set his eyes upon them with envy, and was determined to have them at any price. He had seen them only a short time previous to my taking the room in which they hung, and he seldom passed the wicket without looking in to inquire whether the gardener had come to any decision. He was a pertinacious fellow, who thought that money would do anything, and he was not far wrong. Eventually he came with the money in his hand. He had increased his offer from a crown to one pound five shillings, and this sum, being displayed in small change, seemed a fortune in the eyes of the indigent gardener who, however, still refused to part with his prints, notwithstanding that it was his object to make a provision for old age.

"The room will look nothing without them," said he.

"You cannot eat them," said the money-lender.

"They do my eyes good," replied my landlord.

"But you don't eat with your eyes."

"That's true; but somehow I want things to look at. Somehow I don't want to part with that picture of the girl with the little dog and the pitcher. I picked her up at a sale, and I might never be able to pick up another so cheap. She is but a picture, yet she seems to be one of the family almost. She does look so like a sister of mine that died when I was a child, long ago. She has just the same pretty sulky look, and when I used to plague her, poor girl, she would drop her pretty under lip, just like that. She never went to the spring for water without taking her dog with her. It was a shepherd dog's pup. Father was a shepherd on the Wolds a long way from market town. God bless me, she went without shoes without thinking it strange. Polly had beautiful feet, just like those in the picture. I tell you what, sir, I won't part with her, and there's an end of it."

Such were the kind of meetings which now and then took place between the cotter and the man of loans respecting the engravings which hung in my studio. At length the thing became serious. The money-lender, who was far from entering into the feelings of the gardener, could barely hide his ill temper on being thus baffled in his object. His looks betrayed his evil nature. He had ruined many in his time.

The gardener's wife, with a woman's shrewdness, remarked that "she did not like his eyes." This was when he had left, after the gardener had revived the reminiscence of his boyish home on the Wolds.

"I am afraid he means thee no good," said the wife.

"Maybe not," replied the husband; "but yet, he continued, "I hardly see how he can harm me, I never borrowed of him."

"He may get some other gardener to do up his place," rejoined the apprehensive wife.

"Let him do his worst; but I'll be hanged outright before I part with my prints," was the gardener's answer.

"Curse the pictures," ejaculated the woman, "I wish they had never come into the house."

CHAPTER XXXVI.

THE MONEY-LENDER'S SCHEME.

I OFTEN sat looking at the two engravings after the great stir which they had occasioned. The "Girl with the Pitcher" appeared more touching and irresistible than ever, after what the gardener had said about it. It is the mastery of art so to impress the beholder. I was hardly less struck with the wood scene, with the groups of cows and horses, and the herdsman sleeping in the grass. Its solitary spirit infected me. I, too, in my boyhood, had known such scenes, and lived in them; I might say revelled in them. Gainsborough painted solitude better, truer, than any other artist I have studied. One familiar with rural life, where cottages mingle their roofs with the verdure of the forest, will have noted a slow dreamy way peculiar to retired cottars. When, returned from toil in the field, they sit at the door, or, at early dawn, when they come forth to greet the sun, how vacant they look! How little they resemble ordinary pictures of rustic life! If you want to see portrayed the perfect character of rusticity, you must needs go to Gainsborough. If you want the air of true gentility, go to Gainsborough; nay, if you look for dignity, you may pass by this master and fare worse. There is truth, delicacy, sensibility, and pathos in everything that he touched.

I would have copied the two prints, and so brought matters between the gardener and the money-lender to a settlement. I made several attempts to imitate the expression of the rustic girl's face, in vain. Those who buy copies of Gainsborough's works for originals are easily cheated. I have seen scores make the attempt to copy his graces without success. In one instance alone do I remember anything like an approximation to success, and that was in the case of an artist of great distinction, a great lover of Gainsborough. Even in this case the rose tinge upon the cheeks of the original portrait lost half its spring-like freshness in the process of being transferred to another canvas. In making the attempt myself to copy, I expected to be able to succeed only so far as to satisfy my landlord with the copies that he might be induced to part with the engravings; but when I showed him my best efforts, he only smiled. He wanted the money the engravings would bring, and he would like to please, or rather not to offend, his rich neighbour and customer; but he would not part with his art treasures.

Time went on and the affair was well-nigh forgotten. The money-lender never once referred to the prints. He often came to the cottage with small orders or to give instructions about his flower garden, and appeared so friendly and carried on his intercourse in so natural a manner that even the acuteness of the dame, my landlady herself, was at fault. As the gardener advanced in years, he found the labours of gardening too much for his strength. He often expressed a wish to possess a pony and cart for the removal of gravel or manure, to lighten his own labour and save the expense of cartage, and furthermore to enable him to take his good wife on an occasional visit to a married daughter who lived in a neighbouring hamlet. This wish of my landlord was often expressed, and got to be generally known; yet no one seemed likely to settle the difficulty as to how the money was to be got. My own purse was too low to enable me to advance a sum from eight pounds to ten pounds. We often, when sitting at the door or window, saw pony carts go past, and as often the subject was revived, until at last hardly anything else was talked about. The money-lender's house was built in a green close or paddock nearly opposite, so that we could overlook it from our bedroom windows. Our prosperous neighbour had every convenience in the shape of out-houses and stable for the accommodation of domestic animals: but his taste lay not in that direction. He kept one ferocious dog to guard his property, and no more. Horses and dogs, he used to say, "ate their heads off," and he would have nothing to do with them. We were not a little astonished, therefore, one morning to observe a sturdy pony grazing in our neighbour's close, and moreover very plainly to be seen under a shed was a cart to match. The morning following the money-lender stopped at the cottage as usual to order some cauliflowers for his dinner, but made no allusion to his new acquisition. He had not, however, been gone many minutes, when he came running back, saying that "he had forgotten what he had chiefly called about," which was to ask the gardener, my landlord, to take charge of the pony, as the boy whom he kept in the house was unused to animals. The request was readily acceded to; a second time the pony's master returned, and on this occasion to say that, "as animals ate their heads off unless they were made to work, the gardener if he had any gravel or manure to cart, or in fact any other job, the pony was at his service. Perhaps," he added, "as it is near quarter-day, there might be furniture to remove here and there." Again, for the third time, our neighbour returned to the cottage door, saying, "By the bye, I have heard that you have friends a few miles off in the country. If you would like to pay them a visit on Sunday or week day, it is all one to me—the better the day the better the deed—the pony and cart are at your service always. Of course," he added as he walked on, "I shall expect that you will make no charge for attendance on the animal."

All this was spoken so fairly that no one in the cottage would have suspected an evil intention lurking beneath so many smooth words, had it not happened that the old dame caught another glance of the pony-owner's eyes, who must needs satisfy his curiosity as to the effect which his last offer had made on the gardener. That look had something in it so sinister that when the money-lender was gone, the dame exclaimed:

"I tell thee what, thou shalt have nothing to do with that man, nor his pony, nor his cart, nor anything belonging to him."

"*I, too, tell you what, wife,*" replied the husband, "if you go on at that rate I shall have to pack you off to the Bartle Asylum. Why, woman, what harm can he mean me?"

"Don't *woman* me," retorted the dame, "for I

won't have it. I'll lay my life on't that your friend the money-lender will bring us all to the workhouse before the year's out, and you are Simple Simon enough to buy his pony cart on trust."

CHAPTER XXXVII.

THE PREDICTION OF THE GARDENER'S WIFE PROVES TRUE.

WITHIN a week after the wife's prediction, and without consulting any one, the gardener became the owner of the pony and cart, on the condition that he paid for them by weekly instalments. He had, however, forgotten in making the arrangement that it was just on the approach of winter, when gardeners are usually frozen out. True, he had his weekly wages to receive from the head gardener of the college owning the surburban plantation and shrubberies: but this was a trifle—none too much to fill the cupboard and pay rent. Therefore it came about that the expenses of keeping the pony and paying for it weekly soon drove the gardener into difficulties and arrears with small tradespeople. At first the money-lender did not ask for the Gainsborough prints outright; he merely begged for the loan of them. He then fancied the china, and some of the better articles of furniture, until in the course of the winter he almost emptied the cottage parlour of its most valued contents, and always under the plea that he would return them when the gardener had settled with other creditors. He only took them, he said, in a friendly sort of way, in order to prevent other creditors from making free with them. To make matters worse, the poor gardener, almost beside himself, in order to mitigate his anxiety, took to frequenting a neighbouring alehouse, where cards were not forbidden, and, by combining gambling with drinking, completed the work of ruin so ably commenced by the money-lender. In one of his drinking bouts, which usually lasted several days, he raffled off the pony and cart for about five pounds, being that amount less than the price he had agreed to pay for them. With this sum he thought to pay up arrears of weekly instalments, and to settle all by the loss of the money he had already paid, and so get back his property in pledge. The usurer received the money, but delayed returning any of the goods, making many plausible excuses for his conduct, which by degrees enraged the gardener beyond bounds. Hitherto he had kept his affairs pretty well to himself, but now he grew excited and feverish and took to his bed. Never was poor wretch more utterly powerless to right himself. Luckily the doctor called in was related to the Archdeacon

St. John, one of the old carver's patrons, recently mentioned by me. When the doctor had seen and prescribed for his patient, he came into the parlour to consult with the dame. "Something has occurred," he observed, "to bring about this illness of your husband, and, if it is no very grave secret, I should like to know what it is;" and he proceeded, looking on the now blank wall over the fireplace. "What have you done with the Gainsborough prints I used to admire so much?"

"That's it," replied the wife, wiping her eyes; "those pictures were the cause of all our troubles;" and thereupon she told the whole story of her husband's dealings with the ensnaring money-lender in the most circumstantial manner, laying great stress on her own forethought and wise prediction. The doctor listened patiently—made notes of points of interest, and took his leave. How he proceeded to act none of us knew: but in three days from that time every article of furniture, china, and pictures, including the Gainsborough prints, found their way to the places they formerly occupied. All the explanation we ever had on the subject was that the doctor had stated the case to his uncle; and the Archdeacon was an influential personage of whom the money-lender stood in awe and dread, on account of some malpractices of which he had been guilty in certain dealings with some under-graduates. The cause of the gardener's illness being thus removed, he recovered and went to and fro to the different shrubberies and plantations as before, and grew day by day more and more attached to the Gainsboroughs which he had been so near losing.

CHAPTER XXXVIII.

HIS LORDSHIP'S PORTER.

During the winter I did little besides make what appeared to be fruitless experiments. When, however, spring came, I went sketching in the fields, as I had often done in company with my drawing-master, M. Dalby, whose style I tried hard to imitate, and failed; whose ill-fortune I equally endeavoured to avoid, but without success. My pounds became pence: and then I remember that the May mornings seemed less bright and balmy. The fields put on a sunless, gloomy aspect when the last shilling was gone. Spring is a bad season for the wayfarer. In autumn he may find nuts, berries, crab-apples, acorns, hips and haws, and all manner of sustenance in the wild woods; but in spring the fertile looking fields and forests are to the hungry as profitless as the barren heath. One morning, in hopeless plight, chanced to stray into the vicinity of a nobleman's palace, the Gothic chapel of which had engaged me and my old master some eighteen months in its restoration. It was when his lordship took possession of his estates at his father's death. I was reminded that I might still find a friend within this abode of opulence and refinement, in the person of an ancient steward of the household, whose acquaintance I had made during our labours in the chapel. Having learned at the lodge, however, that the steward had died during the previous winter, I was about to retire, when the little pompous porter, who was seated outside his door, in an antique chair, basking in the sun, opened his small lizard-like eyes (he had answered my inquiry without putting himself to that trouble), and interrogated first himself and then his visitor before him, thus:

"I fancy I know that face?"

"Indeed, sir?"

"'Prentice of the old carver, as did up the chapel?"

"The very same."

"Take a seat."

"Thank you."

"Where have you been so long? What's become of the old carver? Glad to see you.. Old carver dead, eh? Sorry to hear it. What are you doing now? Turned painter? Was thinking about you—was saying I should like to have a little talk with you. Remember, you used to have a genius for drawing; said to Jane only the other day, if I could meet with the old carver's lad, I'd get him to sketch my picture. Fine chair, this, always had a fancy for this chair. Belonged to a lady in the village. Bought it at her sale. I've got a few old paintings. Walk in. You see that with the hole in it—it's reckoned good. Can't think of the master's name. Get my Pilkington's 'Dictionary of Painters,' Jane. Let me see! begins with—ah, well, we'll attend to that presently. What I want to see you about more particularly is my *own* picture. What have you got in the folio? Sketches? Now, what would be about the figure for a whole length? Jane thinks I ought to have my portrait whole length, and I think so too. Been very fortunate. Was only under-butler when the chapel was done up. You remember. Mine's a curious history. Ought to be printed. Seven of us, all boys, bred to the plough; might have been no better all my days but for a very fortunate accident. It's an ill wind that blows nobody any good, as they say. The squire had a son who was badly afflicted, and, in consequence, required some one to keep an eye upon him, wherever he went. Well, the squire tried several lads about, without finding one he could trust. The young squire was constantly falling into some trouble or another, tumbling into a ditch, or over a stile. Well, at last the squire tried me, and from that day the lad began to mend apace, and in the end got quite rid of his ailment, and my services were no longer required. I was just thinking of returning to the plough-tail, when I was sent for to the Manor House, where the squire and his lady received me as if I had been one of the family. They had me into the parlour, just as I was, in my hobnail boots, all on a Turkish carpet, as soft as a feather-bed. Fancy, I had to go right up to the fire-place, and drink the squire's health. 'And now,' says the squire to me, 'Samuel,' says he, 'what can we do for you?' Of course I hardly knew what to say. 'We have been thinking,' says he, 'of recommending you to my lord as a very proper person to fill a vacancy which is open in his buttery. Would you like to be my lord's under-butler, Samuel?' Of course I need not tell you what answer I gave the squire. I took the place, and for seven years I cleaned the knives, forks, boots, shoes, and plate, three hundred and twenty pieces of plate in all, and never lost a bit, not so much as a tea-spoon, and never heard a word of complaint, which of course was very flattering to me, and very much to my credit. Well, that makes the second period of my life. First the ploughboy, and then the under-butler. The young squire grew up and went to college with his present lordship, and they are about as decent a couple of fellows as you would find in a day's march.

Time came when the young squire had it in his power to do me a service, and, without my asking, he used his influence with my lord, and pushed me into the lodge here, which is something like an appointment; and here I am with my wife and two children, about as well satisfied with myself and things in general as any man could well be."

It had been a less infliction to paint the loquacious porter's portrait, gratis, than to have been thus condemned to listen to his ceaseless and discursive story; but the reduced state of my commissariat induced me to endure it.

"I was born fortunate," recommenced the self-complaisant occupant of the arm-chair. "Everything I have tried has turned out well. I bought this carved chair for next to nothing. My small collection of paintings, which I am told is worth the house which holds them, only cost me 7*l.* 15*s.* I joined the Horticultural Society, and, without putting a spade in the ground, got several prizes. There's no such children as mine in these parts; and, though I say it, a better sort of woman than my wife never broke bread. I think, after what I have told you, you will admit I might venture to sit for my portrait."

"Certainly," I replied; and I should have agreed with him on that point without his autobiographic preamble. But he astonished me by drawing upon his smattering acquaintance with pictures, to suggest a few accessories to his portrait, in which prodigal taste he was, perhaps, not so singular as unreasonable.

"Well then," he remarked, "now comes the question as to the style in which the thing ought to be done. If it makes no difference in the charge, I should like to be painted sitting in the old chair, just beside the pillar of the gateway, and with the first quadrangle seen in the background, and through the second archway a glimpse of the park, and just a sprinkling of deer under the oak trees in the distance. I've been looking at a picture of Vandyke's in the library, and I find that you could venture to bring in a curtain hanging down the pillar, and likewise a table with ornamental cover; and if it would not be much more expensive, I've a fine bronze inkstand, which would stand upon the table, quite in character with the chair. Perhaps you would be able to put in a few letters, with one in my hand, and a few pens? The post letters all pass through my hands. Then what do you say to introducing the medals of the Horticultural Society, in the morocco case, together with the various prize-flowers, hollyhocks, and roses of various colours, with the vases in which they were sent to the show? I thought at one time of your throwing in a few pieces of his lordship's plate, just to remind people of the fact of my having had charge of it for seven years, without losing so much as a tea-spoon, and—but that I leave to your superior taste. I don't know how you may be situated, but if it would be worth your while to take the job, I shan't be nice to a few shillings, you can have something in advance. I'll get you permission to his lordship's gallery, where you can make as many copies as you like; and I expect, if you make a good thing of my picture, you will get half the village to paint. But you must do mine cheap for a beginning. What do you say to fifteen shillings, with half the money down at starting?

Of course I felt highly honoured by the liberal proposition of the illustrious gate-keeper; at the same time I did not immediately close with his offer, preferring, for reasons which suggested themselves, to think the matter over for a day or two. The self-conscious Samuel had, unwittingly, put a thought into my head for which I felt rather inclined to think well of him, in spite of his meanness and conceit. On returning home, I thought it best to address myself a letter to his master, requesting permission to study in his gallery. Strange that the idea had never struck me before. It was in this very collection I had formerly studied the two pictures I have referred to, by Van Aelst. The place was literally crowded with gems of the highest value.

In my letter, I recalled to the noble owner's recollection my former services in restoring the Gothic chapel, and briefly remarked how that the death of my master and the decline of the Gothic taste had led me to a change of profession, and begged that he would permit me to copy a few of the smaller works in his cabinet, with the view of improving my hand, and at the same time my finances. The effect of my letter was most unexpectedly cheering. Before I had well set to work in my studio on the following day, a little pony drew up at my door, and a country lad who was employed as messenger at the palace delivered a letter into my hands, giving me access at all times to his lordship's pictures, and permission to copy any number of the same, family portraits excepted. His lordship was further good enough to say that in the course of a month he would be leaving for the continent, but that he had arranged with Mr. R——, the famous restorer, to clean and restore such of his pictures as were thought to need it, and that, if his influence and introduction to the said Mr. R—— would be of any service to me in the way of procuring employment, he should be only too happy to serve me. This was the very opportunity of all others I most desired.

CHAPTER XXXIX.

MADAME MITCHEL'S.

NOT long after my interview with the ambitious porter at the lodge gate, I chanced to stroll into the park, pondering by the way on the state of my finances, which had become critical in the extreme, when I accidentally came upon a gay group assembled near the ornamental water, and at once recognised the youth whom I had known as Laura Bezza's lover sitting conspicuously among the party, beside a wealthy heiress, the daughter of a tradesman in the city. My thoughts at once reverted to the Italian girl. I was surprised not to find her one of the party. A blush passed over the face of the youth, as his glance met mine, and on that instant it occurred to me that there was something meant by that expression of shame. Suddenly, my theme was changed, and all my old thoughts of Laura returned, so that her image haunted me henceforth. Had he forsaken her? Had her poverty chilled his ardour? The breaking up of the old carver's establishment had proved as fatal to the Signor as to myself. I could not account for the absence of the daughter, nor reconcile what I saw. Hitherto it had been some consolation to me to believe that at least the Signorina—she seemed but a child at that time—was beloved by one who had the means to protect her from the cares of poverty. I had lost sight of her since my master's death, but had not forgotten—that were impossible—the bright vision of the garden, and the roses I had plucked from my window on that eventful sunny autumn morning. I resolved that I would not sleep until I had satisfied myself of the fate of the Italian maiden.

In almost every city in England there is some one particular house where foreigners specially congregate. The poorer sort of Italians, Germans, and Hebrews will favour some one tavern, where they can meet to transact business, cook their humble meals, and, after a day of toil, rest themselves in peace. When once a lodging-house of this description is established, it becomes known in every part of Europe, and is sure of success. Economy, strict economy, must be the order of an establishment where wandering Jew pedlers are the chief patrons. Madame Mitchel's was a house of this kind: and she, being a woman of feeling and of honour, was much respected by the Babylonish throng which nightly assembled in her large dingy parlour. Weary and worn, long-bearded men came in at dusk. Among others there was "Old Jacobs," who dealt in precious stones, spectacles, and black lead pencils. He had used the house for half a century. Then there was "Lame Lazarus," who bought paintings and carvings: and I particularly call to mind a venerable widow Jewess. In fact, the majority were poor-looking Hebrews who dealt in every conceivable commodity. Added to this class were some Italians who made plaster figures. These last were more settled in their habits, and would live for many years in the same rooms. When a child, I lived near to this "house of call," and I remember that the long beards and haggard faces of some of the patriarchal wanderers created no small alarm in the juvenile ranks of the locality; but when I saw that they were gentle and harmless, I was filled with respectful curiosity, and I would stand and watch them prepare their fish at the cistern near the stable up the court, or as they passed to and fro, in the dim light of the evening, more like denizens of another world, than inhabitants of this. My career had all along been more or less associated with this dirty old tavern. M. Dalby had once or twice sent me there for casts, and the old carver had kept up a constant connection with the dealers who called there periodically with their relics of the past. And yet out of a population of thirty thousand, perhaps not five hundred of the inhabitants had seen or heard of the dingy "house of call," in its retired "no thoroughfare." I went instinctively to this comfortless habitation in search of Bezza and his daughter. Long known to the respected landlady, I walked boldly into her little bar and inquired if the Bezzas were at home, assuming that they lived there, for fear of denial.

"One moment ago," replied the landlady, "the poor girl Laura was seated beside me here in this little room. The Signor, as usual, is gambling with old Campiani, his countryman, up-stairs. Sometimes he wins, and sometimes he loses; luck has gone against him lately. He works for Campiani in the modelling line: but it happens frequently that he has played away all the money due for his work before his model is finished, and so he goes on. It is a sad life for a young girl to lead."

"What does Laura, all the time?"

"Works like a slave, cleaning moulds and scraping off the seams of the plaster figures after they are cast. I saw her fingers were bleeding to-night, as she sat in that chair in which you are now sitting, with constant handling of the files, glass-paper, and Dutch rush, as they call it. She does bronzing occasionally, but the verdigris is too powerful for her. I knew her mother, just such another beauty as little Laura. She died in my own arms, poor soul. Well, you see, I'm a sort of mother to these people. They keep me poor. Very few of them pay up. They would if they could; but I tell you, if it was not for the little Laura, the Signor would very soon budge from the "Brown Bear," that he would."

"Could I speak with Laura a moment?"

"Certainly; you are a great favourite; she told me so. Do you know that picture?"

True enough—there was my poor imitation of Van Aelst.

"She prizes that picture," continued the landlady, "above all things. That's why it's in my place. She did not say as much, but I know she feels that it is safer here than in her own room. You know what I mean. The signor will play away the coat off his back when the fit is on. When did you see Laura last?"

"I have not seen her for months. I thought she was to be married to the son of the rich mercer on the Mount."

"Ah, the villain! The moment he found she was poor he left her; and he was not content with that, but he must needs insult her on account of her father's faults. But that gave her small concern, and I know why. She had never absolutely promised her heart to the pitiful fellow, and for very good reasons. Perhaps she was wrong in so far that she did not absolutely discourage him."

"Did she love another?"

"Do you love Laura yourself? Come, answer me that."

"That is certainly an answer for other ears," I replied, blushing at being thus abruptly interrogated; but Mrs. Mitchel was too much the mother of her guests, to stand on ceremony.

"Would you reject her because she is poor, or because her father is not what we could wish him?"

"I certainly should love her a thousand times more for her troubles."

"Come along, you shall see her and tell her so. But stop, you are so great a stranger, I will just see her myself first, and ask permission, for she is a fiery little creature, and might be offended with us both."

So saying the kind-hearted woman disappeared along a dark passage, whither my eyes followed her, and a door opening displayed a lighted room, hung about with casts, and there in the midst stood the charming Laura, wan and motionless, as the figure of Diana on which she was at work. Disregarding the good landlady's presence, and precautionary measures, in an instant I stood by the side of the beautiful girl. We said but little, but that little was enough to satisfy Madame Mitchel that her "two favourites" had been too long parted.

From that hour I became devoted to the "classics," of which old Campiani had an endless assortment. I spent my evenings assisting Laura with her work; in other words, I did Laura's work, which to me was nothing difficult, having a good knowledge of modelling, moulding, and casting. The Signor was delighted beyond measure with me; so much so that he actually began to reform apace, and became more attached to his profession. In one respect I had formed an unfair estimate of his worth. He was a much greater artist than the old carver had been willing to allow. His statuettes had an elegance quite rare, and I derived great improvement from the critical reflections in which the Signor frequently indulged upon various sculptors, ancient and modern. Campiani's stock included many casts from original antique fragments, which happened to be fine early impressions, and thus, for the purposes of illustration, were hardly inferior to the sculptures from which they were taken. In this respect, sculpture has the advantage over painting. The most delicate chisel-work can be moulded and cast, and so multiplied; while on the contrary, the finest copy of a master-piece in paint can never approximate very closely to the spirit of the original. The copy will be more or less tame, in consequence of the process of copying. Even copies by the greatest masters, those which are remarkable for freedom of handling—such, for instance, as those Rubens made in his travels in Italy—may be easily detected. Copies by Rubens may be known by their forced freedom amounting to caricature, and are hardly to be preferred to more laboured imitations by inferior hands. Sitting among our remains of the Athenian chisel, the Signor, in his happier moments, would quietly insist upon the superiority of the ancients over the moderns, and point out with his modelling stick the precise features in which that superiority consisted. Raphael, he would say, came nearest in design to the highest examples of the Athenian sculptures, but that even Raphael wanted the fair proportions, unaffected energy, and elegant contour of the more ancient masters. He cited, in support of this assertion, a fragment of the frieze of the Parthenon, and the remains of a Venus. In the frieze, and more especially in the contours of the horses, the sculptor "had strictly adhered to nature in her finest forms." In their mutilated state even it was possible to trace the most accurate knowledge of anatomy. The attitudes were never constrained; while the details—the flesh, veins, and integuments—were indicated with the nicest discrimination. Nothing in the works of the Italian school, he persisted in saying, came near in loveliness to "Niobe's lovely Daughter." This was going far, when we reflect upon the womanly graces of the Madonnas of Raphael; and "it is certain," the Signor would further insist, "that the Belvedere Apollo,

> 'As in graceful act he stands,
> His arm uplifted with the extended bow,'

reigns supreme over all."

It seldom happens that men commence life with the design of becoming connoisseurs. Men of fortune, in most cases, come to be possessed of pictures through accidental circumstances; and it is an equally contingent circumstance if they happen to understand or care anything about them. The wealthy collector associates with men of his own class, who, like himself, are the fortunate owners of works of genius; and thus, by degrees, he obtains a smattering of art-knowledge, so as to be able to enjoy the wonders of the pencil and chisel which adorn the walls and corridors of his mansion. But a very much closer acquaintance with the *modus operandi* of the artist is essential when the purchase of pictures and statues is in contemplation; and if the man of wealth would hope to succeed in his fine-art speculations, he would do well to frequent the studios of the best painters and sculptors. One reason why the great painters and sculptors of old were great was in consequence of the close intimacy which existed between the artist and his patrons, as in the case of Lorenzo de Medici, who set the example of making his palace at once a school of learning and a school of arts. Painters, sculptors, and men of genius, were, in fact, "the court" there. It was the same with the ancients. "The statuaries of Greece," as Daniel Webb observes, "were not mere mechanics. Men of education and literature, they were more the companions than servants of their employers; their taste was refined by the conversation of courts, and enlarged by the lectures of their poets." In the present day such happy unions rarely exist. The artist's life is, commonly, one long struggle. He is worn out before the friendly hand is held out to him. It is owing to the paucity of real connoisseurs that he dissipates his genius and his strength on unworthy, but indispensable, speculations. He who would live to study must study to live, and this necessity is fatal to the experimental discursiveness of genius, which requires opulence of opportunity. Some have asserted that "we are all born judges of art;" but I should say that so far from this being true, there are, on the contrary, thousands of people whom no opportunities will make judges of art. They may see all the galleries in the world, and visit every studio, and never rise beyond the point of being "well informed."

Yes, the gift of connoisseurship no less requires opportunities of cultivation, leisure, experience and devotion; hence the closer union of the patron and the artist would be to the interest of both.

CHAPTER XL.

THE PICTURE RESTORER.

Opie, the Royal Academician, when lecturing at the Academy, addressed some very pertinent remarks to such of his youthful audience who, he suspected, might unhappily have enrolled themselves as art-students without possessing the requisite capacity. He warned them against taking up the pencil with the view of escaping the drudgery of the counting-house. He pictured to them the misery and degradation which would be consequent upon failure. He advised the young man to whom his observations might apply to avoid the Academy as he would "a pestilence," or he might come to skulk through life as a hackney-likeness taker, a copier, a drawing master, or pattern drawer to young ladies; or he even might be driven to "turn *picture-cleaner*," and help Time to destroy excellences which he could not rival. I read and pondered much over this frank and very practical piece of advice, when it happened that I was selected (upon his lordship's recommendation) to aid the London restorer in cleaning the pictures at the palace. Having heard but indifferent accounts of picture-restorers in general, I was agreeably surprised to find my new master an artist of great abilities, devoting his life to the renovation of damaged pictures with the same earnestness that the old carver had displayed in the restoration of dilapidated churches. Considering the vast number of fine pictures which proceeded from the pencil of the sublime old masters, it must at once be evident either that pictures possess immortal juvenescence or picture restorers are indispensable. The active creative artist is not over given to trouble himself with the works of the old painters; he commonly concerns himself with them only in so far as he may profit by their contemplation. The restorer, on the contrary, should be one who, possessing art-knowledge, artistic skill, and genuine love of art, is willing to sacrifice all prospects, fame, and honour as an original artist, to perpetuate the fame of the great dead. With my new employer the restoration and conservation of pictures was a mission. He stood in precisely the same relationship to the old painters as the Gothic carver had stood to the mediæval sculptors. His hand was guided by principle, and his heart and soul were in the work he undertook. The various styles of painting were as familiar to him as the features of his daily acquaintances. It was interesting to hear him describe the injuries and diseases to which the objects of his veneration and care were subject. He had dwelt among old panels and canvases all his life. His father had pursued the same profession before him, so that from infancy he had been familiar with the terms of his craft, and he had thus by degrees acquired a thorough intimacy with the principles upon which the art of painting rests. By dint of much reading, consultation with eminent painters, and long and painstaking investigation, he had succeeded in classifying the beauties and defects of those painters whom he was accustomed to designate his representative masters. His views of art and artists appeared to me much more extensive and liberal than even original artists ordinarily entertain, and for obvious reasons. He could admit into his good graces works curious and rare in their way, which it would be policy to avoid where the formation of a popular style is the object of the students. He could dilate with equal zest upon the quaint, hard, luminous compositions of John Van Eyck, and the graces and subtile transitions of light and shade of Correggio. Not that he assumed to understand or to care for all the styles of painting; but he had really mastered and was deeply interested in the leading styles which at various times have characterised this noble art. He was in judgment and in liberality an accomplished connoisseur. I was only too glad to place myself under such a man, in preference to remaining a mere "hackney-likeness taker." My own experience as a restorer had, as I have explained, been confined to wood and stone; but then I had not wholly neglected the art of painting. At the very outset of my career in the capacity of picture-restorer, my master found me neither incompetent nor inapt, while every day added to my knowledge and consequent usefulness.

The previous owner of the princely residence where we were engaged, had remained through life what nature had designed him to be—to wit, an admirable steady-going country gentleman. He had regarded his pictures in the light of harmless dead stock, which neither ate nor drank; he saw them daily and hourly, but it never occurred to him that they needed the appliances of art to preserve them. He had critical sagacity in all matters pertaining to husbandry. Live stock he could contemplate with the eye of an experienced grazier. More, he was proud of his tenantry and kind to his labourers. But, meanwhile the Raphaels, Titians, and Correggios, abandoned to neglect, were silently undergoing the ordinary process of decay consequent thereupon, and were soon to become (for all our titled farmer cared to the contrary) the mere ashes of splendour, and rubbish of elegance and beauty. The grandfather of his present lordship had also manifested great capacity and a noble disposition as a landowner, but he was equally neglectful of his pictures. He, however, while possessing little regard for well-stocked farms, betrayed the utmost indifference for the *chefs-d'œuvre* of the old masters. It was his ambition to be foremost in the ranks of ornamental gardeners, and he might be said to care most for whatever came under the head of gardening. Grottoes, fountains, gold and silver fishes, choice exotics, and variegated birds, were with him absorbing objects of attention. These were to him health, life, fame and happiness. But while his gardens presented to the eye the aspect of fairy land, the pictures in the gallery remained in the gallery unregarded. Works of men pre-eminently gifted, a study for the most exalted intellects, were forgotten in their noble owner's passion for horticulture. In consequence of all this neglect on the part of his lordship's predecessors, we found plenty to do in the palace; nearly every work of art required renovation more or less.

Some of the Italian masterpieces, being executed upon a soft, spongy wood, similar in its nature to lime-tree, had been half consumed, as far as the panels were concerned, by the slow ravages of an insignificant worm, so that in each instance, the surface, or the paint—that is, the picture—needed transferring, an operation requiring great care and delicacy of handling. It was my early task to remove the remaining portions of decayed timber from the back of these pictures, for which task my experience in wood and sharp-edged tools had qualified me in no ordinary degree. This was especially fortunate, as on this account I at once made good wages, which I much needed. But for my skill in this department, it would have been necessary to have risked sending the pictures in question to London. Stop saws, chisels, planes, pieces of glass, files, steel scrapers, grit, and solvents, are some of the means employed in "transferring," and I was tolerably conversant with the handling of these various instruments. It is not generally known that the finest pictures in Europe have been thus transferred from wood to canvas, as the only means of saving them from utter ruin. The French restorers appear first to have ventured upon this ingenious and delicate expedient in the case of some Raphaels and Titians which had decayed to the last extremity. The surface of the picture to be operated upon is protected by layers of paper. These are pasted on, and finally a coarse gauze is added. When dry, the picture is fastened, face downward, on to a smooth bench, and the decayed timber cut, planed, scraped, and ground away, until only the coating, about the thickness of a wafer—that is the picture itself—remains. One or two canvases, some inches larger than the picture, are then carefully and smoothly cemented to the back surface thus presented. When dry, the painting is then taken up from the bench, and strained upon a stretching frame, just as if it were a picture painted upon canvas; and the paper being moistened and removed from the front of the work, the process is completed. Many an invaluable painting has by this process obtained a new lease of its existence. We know that fifty years will go far to destroy the canvases upon which our masterpieces depend for support, and that it has only been by cementing the worn-out canvases upon new ones that we are now in possession of the majority of our finest pictures. "Cleaning," "stopping," "stippling," "lining," "transferring," "cradling," "battening," and "veneering," are only a few of the terms which express the several operations of the restorer's art. Of course mechanical operations, such as I have attempted to describe, may be performed without a profound knowledge of the design and colouring of the picture; but the case entirely alters in respect to the restorer's qualifications when the picture has to be freed from darkened oils, repaints, and varnishes. No one should presume to employ either friction or solvents upon the surface of a fine picture without long previous training. This is not the same as saying no one should go into the water until he has learned to swim. There are innumerable indifferent pictures and sign-boards upon which the student might be permitted to exercise his noviciate hand; and when he is careful and successful with unimportant examples, he may be permitted to practise upon works of importance which ascertained skill alone has a right to touch. But, after all, there are but few whom the most careful training would make competent restorers; and there is no making rules for those upon whom nature has showered her choicest gifts. Great natural genius will succeed where mere talent, with no matter how much experience, would signally fail. In some respects there is an analogy between the aims of the restorer and the engraver. It should be the chief pride of the engraver to reproduce as faithfully as possible the several peculiarities of a painter's works; and it is the purpose of the restorer to understand those peculiarities, in order that while treating the surface of the picture he may not injure it. Marc Antonio engraving under the eye of Raphael, rendered that master's pictures with so much skill as to lose very little of their noble character. The restorer should always work as though the eye of the master were upon him. Many who have attempted to engrave

Raphael have paid too little regard to his style, and piqued themselves too much upon making fine showy prints. The restorer must know better than commit this fault. The careless and ill-informed engraver merely confounds or misrepresents the master, but the tasteless, or unprincipled or incompetent restorer destroys the picture. Hence while for the glory of art it would be well for engravers to copy the style of great masters, instead of inventing styles of their own, it is of far greater importance that the picture-restorer should study to understand, in order that he may religiously conserve the works of genius entrusted to his care.

Such were some of the precepts and principles which my employer, the London restorer, enforced and practised.

CHAPTER XLI.

THE TWO RUYSDAELS.

My strength and my prospects lay in the aptitude which I betrayed for the work of restoration. It was, I found, no light matter to satisfy the judgment of the numerous connoisseurs who visited our studio in the palace during the latter part of our stay. By arrangement, the first year (we were two years in all at the work) was spent in the renovation of the larger picture galleries, and in repairing a painted ceiling and staircase which had gone well-nigh to ruin. The gems of the cabinet were reserved until the noble owner's return from the continent, accompanied by some friends who had the reputation of being eminent critics in matters of art. In all the difficulties of the undertaking I was always permitted to be present, and to take part in the delicate and interesting operations to be performed; and each day my employer grew more and more confident of "making an artist of me," and he predicted for me an eminent career, provided I courted it in the metropolis. We found the pictures, one and all, very much in the same dull, monotonous state to which they had been reduced by their long neglect. For half a century had the damp mists of autumn penetrated the rooms, had settled upon the surfaces of the pictures, and absorbed each particle of dust, until it was no longer possible to distinguish the glowing colours of the Flemish and Venetian masters from the sombre and pallid hues of the Spanish school. If possible, the smaller cabinet pictures were even more obscured than the larger and more imposing treasures of the gallery. Among a hundred other examples, by Flemish and Dutch artists, were a pair of sea-pieces by the two Ruysdaels, which had a sort of European reputation. It was by special desire that Sir R—— was present during the process of cleaning these two pictures. In their obscure state they might have passed with tolerably good judges as specimens from one and the same pencil; alike in the character of their subjects, both having passed through the same ordeal under time's mellowing hand; they were of a kindred complexion—to wit, a murky mellowish brown. This tint was spread equally over the entire pictures, producing an effect similar to that which smoked glass would produce if placed betwixt the eye and natural objects. By some of his lordship's friends this dismal tone was declared to be "superb." Old Lord E—— pronounced it to be the true "golden."

"Golden it may be," said Sir R——; "but there is no legitimate excuse for its presence on these pictures."

"You would not, Sir R——; think for one moment of disturbing the mellow warmth of those Ruysdaels?"

"I would recommend that this unsightly varnish and dirt be removed, in order that we may contemplate the pictures in the condition in which the master left them, as nearly as possible."

"But *that* is the original, natural tone, is it not?"

"On the contrary, it is almost as unlike the colour of Jacob Ruysdael, as white is to black."

"You astonish me, Sir R——."

"I see no reason for astonishment, my lord."

"Indeed, I always understood that this mellow warmth, or glazing, which you condemn, was the glory of an old picture. I should like you to explain more fully, Sir R——, before the destructive process for removing it proceeds, what wonderful effects you can expect to obtain by its removal."

"I promise you effects perfectly natural. You will observe, my lord, those breakers on the foreground rocks are of the same tint as the smaller waves in the middle distance, and that the silken flags of the remote vessels are as legible as those which are nearer at hand. How do you reconcile this want of gradation in a master remarkable for realizing the most subtle variations and transitions of light, shade, and tint?"

"I would rather that you continued your explanations, Sir R——, and you will oblige us much by being very definite."

"Very good, my lord. This water, which reminds one strongly of mud, ought to be beyond question, transparent in the shaded portions; the foam wants motion, and the billows have lost form, grace and rotundity. I will explain to you why those flags in the midst of the ocean are as prominent as those which are near. Jacob Ruysdael, like all great artists modelled his distances firmly in solid colour, and the brush-marks have become filled with dirt, varnish, and oil, which, having become darkened, have perverted the master's intention entirely; in fact, we have now a yellowish brown for what was once a delicate grey. I have scarcly ever seen a fine landscape in which the distances were not obscured and confounded by discolourations of this sort. Our own Wilson's pictures are instances in which the remote objects are loaded with colour in such a manner as to collect and retain dust, dirt, and superfluous varnish and oil. The air-tints—the aërial perspective, which commonly is the charm of a landscape, is entirely eaten up by these corrupt glazes."

"But coming more directly to the Ruysdaels under notice, Sir R——, pray inform us as to what good we are to expect from the removal of these time-honoured 'glazings.'"

"I will ensure you more space, air, and light—greater variety in form and colour—and a multitude of details touched in with lightness, precision, and truth, which are now buried in oblivion. Beneath yon overhanging cloud the sea shall look dark and gloomy—a track of sunlight will illumine the distant sails, and reveal the silken flags, crimped and fluttering in the breeze, as if they were endowed with life and motion."

"Enough, Sir R——, we know you for a great connoisseur; as far as I am concerned, you have full license to do your worst."

This discussion on picture-cleaning was attentively listened to by the noble owner of the pictures, who, not possessing much critical knowledge on the subject, was only too pleased to raise discussions so interesting to him as the possessor of art-treasures. Sir R—— had reigned supreme in our *atelier* until the arrival of his venerable opponent, who differed from him on all occasions. Lord E—— was a veritable relic of the old school of *cognoscenti*, who were great sticklers for rust, mildew, and dirt, and who thought pictures and statues very "much enhanced by age and decay." Sir R—— spoke with the authority of one who had paid attention to the subject, and calculated the advantages which accrue to art from restorations judiciously conducted. It transpired in the end, however, that my master, the manipulator, was better informed on the subject in dispute than his illustrious advisers. I said that the two Ruysdaels strongly resembled each other in tone and subject: but it remained to be seen that they were not so nearly allied when regarded as works of art. They had always passed for a pair, and had cost the same amount of money. The observations of the two critics, although pointed especially to one picture, were understood to refer to both; but, on my master receiving instructions to clean them, he took the liberty of telling Sir R—— that the two works, seemingly so much alike, were in reality by different hands—the one being by Jacob Ruysdael, the other by his brother Solomon. At first, this announcement created some astonishment and doubt in the mind of Sir R——, but he was speedily converted when the two productions were placed in juxtaposition, and underwent a minute investigation."

"This is no very flattering discovery," he exclaimed, turning to the owner. "The pictures must be cleaned notwithstanding."

"I can recover all the effects you have enumerated,

Sir R——, in the one case," said the restorer; "but I must forewarn you and my lord that no such beauties are to be found in the imitation."

"True," returned Sir R——; "but you will find I anticipate a relative degree of excellence in it."

"I must tell you, Sir R——, that I have no hope of finding any beauties whatever in the imitation. It is not only painted by an inferior hand, but, moreover by an inferior process. It is in the knowledge of the means and the methods employed by the old masters that the success of our operations in a large measure depends. We know that Jacob Ruysdael painted *his* pictures carefully and honestly, manifesting great discernment in the choice of his 'ground tint.' It was owing to this precaution that his works retain so much of their early natural freshness. Solomon, on the contrary, possessing none of the feeling or ambition, had none of his brother's anxiety for the goodness and durability of his productions. Solomon aimed at the rapid manufacture of an article resembling in leading features his brother's masterpieces. He painted, for instance, on a dark 'ground,' for the sake of the facility it afforded, and the consequence is, that his counterfeits have become blackened by time, while his brother's thoughtful and conscientious compositions have still a grey, mineral-like solidity. The brownish tinge on the Jacob Ruysdael is occasioned by an incrustation upon the surface, which can be removed; while, in contradistinction, the blackness in the example before us, by Solomon Ruysdael, is a radical defect, and utterly incurable."

"Just as I have always asserted," cried Sir R——, when my master had thus expressed his opinion; "these odious films upon old pictures are as favourable to your imitators as night and darkness are to burglars."

"What, then, would you advise under present circumstances?" inquired the owner, of my employer.

"My advice, my lord, is, that you permit me to restore the true picture, and that you dismiss the counterfeit to some other room; but previously to your carrying out this sentence, should you desire it, I will convince you of its justice."

After a lapse of a few days, the genuine picture, the Jacob Ruysdael, shone forth in its original state, very natural, and very beautiful. It was now a picture which not only the learned connoisseur, but even the humblest spectator also could admire and understand. No such transformation took place in the counterfeit. After many unavailing attempts to get at its supposed beauties, it was formally dismissed to a modester chamber.

But to return to my personal affairs. My employer fortunately brought with him his family. From the first, he manifested so much concern for my welfare, that I soon seized an opportunity of telling him the history of my love for the Italian girl, with which he was much interested, and he considerately introduced Laura to his wife and family, who received her with every possible kindness. In fact, no sooner had Laura set foot in the village, than the whole population, numbering some seventy individuals, old and young, declared spontaneously in her favour. Had she made her first appearance in that rural district, graced with the wings of an angel, she could hardly have created a greater sensation. Visitors came from all parts to view the pictures and statues, and had familiarised those humble people with fair faces enough, but still, one and all seemed taken with the fine presence of the beautiful girl from over the sea. Even pompous Samuel, his lordship's porter, opened his small eyes, and left his carved chair, when Laura passed through his gate, and ventured his opinion on the state of the weather and prospects of the harvest in a manner meant to be exceedingly polite. The rustics vied with each other in presenting the new favourite with the choicest of their flowers. Dame Britton sent in a parcel of honey: old Tom, the hedger and ditcher, left a yellow-beaked blackbird in a wicker cage: the children opened all the gates gratis: and, to crown all, the old housekeeper at the Abbey, a very grave personage, invited the "foreign young lady" to tea.

I had now long acquired that feeling of security

and independence which the consciousness of possessing a fair share of practical ability imparts. The Signor (Laura's father) had resumed his usual habits of modelling statuettes and gambling. We sometimes met, and he always expressed unbounded confidence in whatever I did or proposed to do. "Laura's visits to the village," he said, "were peculiarly agreeable to him," and that he was "much affected by the kind reception she had met with. A happy improvement, too, in her health was manifest since her change of life—not that she had ever really been ill; only close toil and long watching over her father's strange and desperate career had begun to imprint upon her face marks of care.

CHAPTER XLII.

LAURA BEZZA.

There was no longer any question, nor any doubt to raise a question that Laura was mine. The Signor entertained no other idea, and, as for Madame Mitchel, she always received us in the light of young people about to be married, and talked of little else beside the coming ceremony. But then came the difficulty of finding a home with little means on hand, with also very undefined prospects, and moreover that greatest of difficulties, the Signor himself. To suppose that Laura would ever forsake her father, however fallen he might become, would have shown an utter want of insight into her character. I who had learned to read her thoughts in her face could not be deceived on this point. It was for this very devotion to her parent that I most of all loved her; and when I found her pale and her dark eyes dilated with grief, I knew that the sharp rattle of the dice-box might be heard on the stairs. At such times her thoughts would wander away, and Madame Mitchel and myself talk on unheeded by her side. Meanwhile her ear was on the stretch to catch the faintest echo of her father's voice, which ever and anon resounded through the house indicating his good or evil luck: sometimes in peals of laughter or bacchanalian song, or, as the mood directed, in exclamatory curses. At intervals, when the last stake was lost, the Signor would resume his work: and gazing on his noble presence as he sat by the lamplight modelling his statuettes, no one would suppose they beheld the man of yesternight waiting with blanched face the turn of the dice. Then in those hours of peace, when every word of the artist's tongue was a wise one—what a change passed over the daughter's countenance! Often have I seen her weep for joy, and her eyes—wont to express anguish, doubt, and fear—flash with delight, and their dark lashes open and shut fan-like, as the butterfly basking in sunlight plays sportingly with its wings. It was delightful to watch this pair, the artist and his child, when thus employed, the father in works of fancy and creation, the daughter in the humbler task of preparing plaster casts for the shops and street vendors: and great was my happiness in sitting by Laura's side taking my share in the work. But what pleased me most of all was the perfect confidence which these exiles had in myself, humble as I really was, considered as an artist: in comparison with Signor Bezza I was but an infant in attainments; and as for the daughter, her beauty and her manners alike fitted her to shine in the palaces whence her kindred had been driven. If I had but one wish it was that I might serve her; and she knew my mind so well that I had never any fear of hidden griefs. Her heart was mine; to me she told her sorrows; to me she came for help always, and hence I knew she loved me. I was with her in happy hours, and I was present when no happiness was hers. She looked for me, depended on me and on no one else, save that in Madame Mitchel we both found a common friend and mother.

And Madame Mitchel told pretty anecdotes of the Signor, of Laura's mother, and of Laura herself. She told how shy Laura was, when but a child she first came with her parents to the inn: how at first she would barely show her face half hidden in raven ringlets behind the half-open door: and how she lisped her own pretty language in her own pretty way: and then how she would venture down a flight of stairs and peep into the bar parlour, and speak her two or three small English words, and fly away with her sweet silvery laugh: and how, as time went by, she made herself understood in little matters: and then how her mother died and left the poor

Signorina in her (Madame Mitchel's) charge altogether, and how she took the child to her breast, to her own bed, and washed and dressed her, as if she had been her own child, and taught her her alphabet, and to read little stories: and how the tiny thing wrote a story in imitation of those she read, about a little girl who was born poor and came to be a princess and would plague Madame to get it printed like other books. Then came the parting, when Laura went to live in the old carver's cottage, where Madame visited on a Sunday, after evening service, to take tea; but that was very seldom, for the inn was always overflowing with foreigners who came, as I have said, from all parts of Europe, and were constantly going in and out, sometimes staying but an hour to rest. And as real treasures, diamonds, pearls, works of art and genius never weary, but grow more and more precious, the more they are looked at and understood, so, day by day, did the beautiful Laura grow more and more precious to me until it appeared that every object in the world beside was as nothing in comparison with her in whom no blemish could by any possibility be found.

CHAPTER XLIII.

THE CATASTROPHE AND THE FLIGHT.

My forebodings were too well founded. The cloud at length burst. Bezza, as I gleaned from Madame Mitchel, became more and more addicted to gaming. An addition had been made to the number of his friends (?) in the person of a Polish gentleman, a teacher of languages. The absence of Laura left her father even more license than he had been accustomed to take while she resided wholly in the tavern. He now, to use the old carver's words, literally turned night into day. The Pole was of a good family: but having rendered himself obnoxious to the despotic rulers of his own country (which ought to be considered something in his favour), he sought refuge in England, and procured a pittance by teaching the language of his fathers to the stranger who gave him shelter and protection. He took up his abode at the "house of call," with others of his countrymen. Here he found no scope for the display of many noble qualities which he assuredly possessed. Excitement offered itself in the dice-box; he found sympathy in Bezza; their misfortunes had originated in the same cause, and they sought solace in the same vice. What crime will not poverty, loneliness, and despair lead to? He came one night and staked his last shilling. The game ran high. He won back in an hour the losses of a week; he had come prepared with false dice. Aroused to watchfulness, his rival's keen glance detected the villany, and denounced it in no measured terms. Then those two men, who had often met as friends, became hateful in each other's eyes, and soon keen words gave way to keener weapons. It chanced I was with Madame in her little bar, talking over the prospects of my speedy marriage with Laura, when the alarm was raised. I hurried up-stairs, but all too late. The Italian passed me with pallid face, and still grasping the dagger. I found the Pole attended by old Lazarus, who, it appeared, happened to be at hand the moment of the quarrel. The wounded man was perfectly cool and collected. His first and only care was to ascertain whether the alarm had spread, for the affrighted Jew had shouted "ten thousand murders." Madame Mitchel came up, and the Pole conjured her by all that was sacred to shut her doors, so as not to allow a breath of what had transpired to escape. He would not he said, have Bezza molested for the wide world. He had himself given provocation, and then sought to hide his fault by appealing to the knife.

"That is all very good, and very well, my dear sir," broke in the Jew; "but if you should die and the officers come, they will make *me* know all about it."

"I have taken care of that," said Madame; "you may make yourself perfectly easy on that score. If you have any regard for me, my house, or the Signor Bezza, don't utter a syllable about what you have seen. We have had noise enough; now let us see what it all amounts to."

The Pole had been bred to the medical profession, and was enabled to calm our fears with some show of authority. He assured us that, although the wound was very painful, it was not more dangerous than the prick of a needle. Notwithstanding, Madame procured lint and bandages enough to stock a hospital, and, by instructions from the patient himself, the injured part was dressed, he all the time watching the progress of the operation through a looking-glass, with a sort of interest he might have felt had he himself been operating upon some other person. The dagger had glanced from a rib and lacerated the left arm. The wound .on the breast looked terrible at first sight, but, upon investigation, turned out to be a mere abrasion. That night I insisted upon taking up my quarters in the patient's room, in order to pay him any attentions of which he might stand in need. I felt how much depended on his recovery, and essayed to hide from myself the gloomy consequences which would follow upon his death. I tried to sleep; but the red spot upon the breast grew larger and more terrible to contemplate in my dreams. Before the dawn of morning I stole softly to the patient's side, and, finding him calmly sleeping, I again lay down, and tried to lull my fears. This time I was more successful. It was broad daylight when I awoke, and this time to find myself alone in the room. The Pole had flown no one knew whither. In the confusion, consequent upon this discovery, I did not observe, while looking about for an explanation, that I held one in my hand. A slip of paper fell from my fingers on the floor which revealed all. It ran thus:—

"Keep the affair of last night secret. I am on the track of Signor Bezza. It is my hope to find and bring him back: and spare the sufferings of his daughter. If I find him not, adieu; I shall never return."

I sought Madame Mitchel and showed her the note, inquiring with some foreboding for the father and daughter, only to learn that they had left on the over night, and that they had done so by Madame Mitchel's advice, backed by the persuasion of old Lazarus. They packed up, and departed by the night coach to London, where they hoped to find means of leaving the country altogether. Madame had informed the Pole of this intention, and hence his sudden pursuit. The generous landlady had provided the means of flight, "wishing and hoping for the best," to use her own words when she beheld my grief. "It is best for you," she observed, "for Laura, for the Signor, for myself, for he has well-nigh borrowed all the money I had in the house." In spite of my own limited means, I could not help feeling for Madame Mitchel. The work of restoration at the palace had concluded. Nothing remained for me but to follow the Italians, whom the Jew said he could find easily: that they were not likely to leave London, for want of money, before we could overtake them. Taking 20*l.*—all my savings —I paid Madame Mitchel half that sum on Laura's account, and set out with the Jew for London. If any man could find the fugitives, that man was Lazarus. I proposed taking the coach in order to hasten our speed: but the Jew told me I was out of my mind; that there was no need of hurry; that he had places to call at by the way: and his "by the way" meant every town, village, and farm-house within sight of the turnpike road. Often, to my disgust, he would ascend an eminence, and cast his eyes over the vale, and whenever a remote church spire was beheld he would arrange a digression there, and sigh, and wish that the place was more near at hand.

CHAPTER XLIV.

SIGNOR ALTOVITI.

Lame Lazarus rented, among others, a large house in Hatton Garden, and in the back premises and upper rooms he had accumulated every conceivable class of goods which go by the common name of "antiquities." These, for the most part, were huddled and heaped together without the slightest regard to order or care—for it was part of his plan to keep objects which were old and decayed in that condition, and to impart to new productions the appearance of age. Upon shelves he had hoarded up broken china and bronzes; tables were strewn with medals and coins; about the floor lay rotten panels and canvases, which revealed grim countenances, dimly visible, and all manner of hideous subjects, looking so vague and unearthly that the manner and means by which they were created could by no possibility be guessed. All the various styles of painting and diverse subjects were sunk into one level obscurity, bordering closely upon oblivion. "Speculative" was the term applied to these commodities. In a loft above he had also stored an immense assortment of carvings, armour, and tapestry of all kinds, and all alike rotten, stained, tattered, battered, rusted, and tarnished by design no less than by the wear and tear of years. Darkness and dirt, however, were reserved for the rubbish. No one knew better than my friend Lazarus how to bring out and set off to advantage the beauties of a really artistic production. Good pictures were revived and put into costly frames, and exquisite bits of porcelain, protected by glass shades. Our collector had in his employ able artists, such as carvers in marble, menders of china, who could model missing bits of crown Derby or old Worcester with great nicety, or create and fit an absent limb to a figure in a way quite imperceptible to the ordinary eye. To these workers he paid very little money, while he abused them very much in slack seasons, telling them that he got nothing by their labours, that all his profits were derived from the inferior articles on which no restorations were made.

It was intended to place me with the carvers; but about the time of my arrival in London the Jew was doing a great stroke of business in pictures, and, therefore, much to my gratification, he placed me in the department for the restoration of old paintings, amid all the paraphernalia of the craft, and under the guidance of an accomplished artist, whom the master with his usual shrewdness had selected to work on the masterpieces. This man was a native of Florence, named Altoviti, a young and extremely handsome man, who wore the best of clothes and displayed a fine taste in jewellery, all in a marked contrast with the principal of the establishment. But, above all, Altoviti was, at least in outward appearances, of a happy disposition, beholding all things in glowing colours, and making sport of circumstances which might have produced quite an evil influence upon less sanguine natures. He kept a guitar always in tune by his side, and would often beguile a few moments in singing his country's songs. Where he was it was no easy matter to be dull. Yet he was not without feeling for those who were unhappy. It was strictly ordered by Lame Lazarus that the Signor, his "great gun," as he called him, should work alone and hold no manner of intercourse with the inferior people about the house; that, above all, he was not to make cheap the secrets of the art by which he imparted the glow of youth to the decayed works of the early masters. So far, however, from carrying out these injunctions of the mercenary Hebrew, the Italian, being fond of company, liked to have in his studio everybody about the house; so that we had concerts, and conversaziones, mostly when the master was abroad, which was daily. Besides, being a real artist, he treated with contempt all idea of secrecy in his mode of working, for he knew very well that we could no more mimic the graceful strokes of his pencil than rival the exquisite strains of his fine voice, which he poured forth with so much fervour that even Lazarus himself could not always resist them. The artist seemed to do very much as he liked with the dealer. He often caricatured him on the wall, and it was wonderful with what good-humour the victim resigned himself to those satirical freaks. The principal's nose and under lip were considerably larger than ordinary. These salient features appeared in the caricaturist's transcript multiplied by twelve, with an aspect hideously droll. For the matter of these wall pictures, we all shared alike; the wilful, wanton satirist spared not even himself. His broad, manly chest exaggerated became the breast of a stout turkey cock, in the style of which bird the Signor was pleased to caricature himself. Sometimes, indeed, the Jew would rage and storm in bad Italian, but this only added to the fun, for then the tormentor would seize a stick and limp up and down the room in perfect imitation of the Jew, and on those occasions there was no help for it, every one laughed outright; even the master himself caught the infection, and laughed until the tears rolled down the furrows of his sallow cheeks. But then, as Lazarus said, the Tuscan was his right hand, a mine of wealth, a fortune. Besides, he was in the Jew's power, and was coaxed and treated better on this account, for the Jew liked to have people in his power. The Jew discounted his bills, sold him jewellery, rings for his own taper fingers, and brooches, bracelets and lockets for his friends, to whom they were appropriate, of whom the Italian had a host. In myself, the good-humoured foreigner found a subject of pleasantry second only to the Hebrew. My provincial aspect took him quite aback. He had never counted, he said, upon seeing anything so matchless as the cut of my coat; my stooping figure and round shoulders, acquired by too much sitting, qualified me for his "Gobbo." Yet while he satirized he was partial to me, and instructed me in the principles of a beautiful art, a sure way to win my gratitude and affection.

Signor Altoviti, while he made sad havoc of the English language in general, had by some means picked up many idiomatic expressions which he used effectively enough. For instance, he was pleased sometimes to designate himself as "a cobbler of old pictures." But while he thus spoke with levity of the calling in which he excelled all others, he was, notwithstanding, jealous of his art, and sensitive in all matters in which artists are most sensitive. "I am a cobbler," he would say, "I botch pictures." In company he would not hear himself called an artist without contradiction. At times he was wont to say that he felt inclined to creep under the table when the imputation was made. In happier moments, however, he would dilate upon the subtleties of the art, which he had mastered, in such a way as to make his hearers believe almost that the restoration of damaged pictures required far greater accomplishments than were usually possessed by the creative artists themselves. To me, at least, he made it well-nigh appear that the old masters painted to obtain the honour of having their pictures restored by Signor Altoviti. When a great picture came into his hands which had been tampered with by some amateur or housekeeper, his rage knew no bounds. Flemish and French pictures he either did not understand or despised. When he spoke of Florentine and Roman design, and Venetian colour, he was as grand and delightful as he was practical. He taught me how certain colours had faded, and how others which looked faded were corroded by oils. In the secret of Venetian colouring he was profound. It was wonderful to watch the blackened canvases resume their ancient splendour, as he passed, in rapid succession, the well-chosen solvents over their long-neglected surfaces. He knew what he was seeking, he would say, and he knew when he had found it. More especially he had a remedy for one particular colour, a warm green, which is to be found only in Venetian pictures, and which in uncleaned pictures of that school always appears as a dark rich liquorish brown. The crust on this colour is found to consist of an oil varnish glaze, which time has darkened and corrupted as we find it. No mild ordinary remedy will remove this incrustation, for it is found so hardened that the sharpest steel instrument will barely raise it. Yet in the twinkling of an eye Signor Altoviti would remove it, by means which in less skilful hands would have left the canvas bare. Genius in restoration, as the highest skill in surgery, will as assuredly triumph as mere talent will as assuredly fail. And Altoviti was pleased to instruct me, and thus by degrees I progressed in my studies, and gave promise of becoming a second Altoviti myself—at least, so said my instructor, who could pay a compliment even better, if that were possible, than he could renovate an injured masterpiece of art.

CHAPTER XLV.

FORLORN HOPES.

MEANWHILE the months went by, and I could gain no intelligence of Signor Bezza and his daughter. The Jew had never any leisure to be spoken to on other subjects than those connected with the business ever immediately before him—his money-getting. He preferred to speak of mending broken vases, to any speculative repairs of broken hearts. When he thought he was unheard, I have listened to him apostrophising the fragments of what had perhaps once been a noble piece of Sèvres ware, in words as fervent in tone and as full of distress as any lover would call to his aid. Now dilating upon the proportion, texture, and tints, of the thing, as if it had appeared to his eye before accident had reduced it to ruin; then lamenting over the worthless shattered remains, until he would work himself almost to frenzy. Yet it was not because he cared for fine proportions, glowing colours, and soft textures of glaze that he grew excited, but because he could not re-unite the fragments of the work, which, when whole, had represented so many hundred francs. Greed of gain and love are worn topics, and what can be said that is new on the subject of hopes deferred?

Night after night, when shops were closed, and often in the rain, I lingered in the dismal streets of Clerkenwell, or wandered about the purlieus of Saffron and Back Hills. Wherever the voice of an Italian might be heard, there might I be seen staring about me like one lost, until I became familiar with all the strolling musicians and image-makers in those parts. The poorest boy with only a white mouse in a box, or a monkey under his jacket, became of more than common regard in my eyes because he spoke in a language which, little as I understood it, was musical and dear to me. I often parted with my hard-earned money to these wanderers, on their return to Clerkenwell sometimes as late as midnight, to purchase a little delay and talk with them in such broken and disjointed manner as I was able, until, after many attempts, I made them, as I thought, comprehend, and how often was I deceived in supposing that they did understand me! What was the object of all these nightly watchings and questionings? Every figure lurking about in court and alley would seem to take the forms of those I sought. My eyes would follow some more than commonly attractive girlish shape as it went tripping by until night and darkness swallowed it up and left me alone; when in my room I have thrown my weary body on the boards, where I slept like others who were as poor as myself, and would still in imagination pursue my search, and continue my fruitless watchings and inquiries. No wonder Signor Altoviti called me his "Gobbo."

I have said that Altoviti appeared happy. Yet I sometimes fancied that I detected sadness in the tones of his voice. It was so. By degrees he grew less joyous, and then I noticed that he ceased to joke upon my gait, clothes, and pensive look, which he had been accustomed to say were particularly droll. Once or twice, while I was at work, I noticed that he sat eyeing me as if with some personal interest, and afterwards, strangely enough, his caricature of me in chalk disappeared from the studio wall, where it had often provoked a smile. I attached no importance to this circumstance. It did not occur to me then that once before in my life an incident precisely similar in respect of the caricature had worked a great impression on my mind, and brought about a happy change in my affairs, and influence on my future life.

CHAPTER XLVI.

THE PRINT COLLECTOR.

The Jew, I have said, was accustomed to abuse his workmen in slack times, and pay them little even when he most needed their aid, and this may be explained by the fact that our peculiar and obscure kind of occupation was only to be obtained from a few houses, and these were scattered about and little known. When work fell off, our hours of labour were reduced, as a matter of course, and, as a matter of course, our wages also. To this rule Signor Altoviti formed the sole exception in the Jew's establishment. He always made full time, and received full pay, not because the Jew loved him one whit more than he loved others, but simply because the town perhaps contained but one Altoviti in the art of picture restoration; and therefore, if the Jew had once parted with him, he might not have been able to fill his place when first-class work came in. In these times of leisure some of the hands stayed about the house, and amused themselves in ordinary ways, to while away the time, while they went into debt for board and lodgings; others, myself among the number, found out little expedients for earning the means of existence. A few doors round the corner, in a small street, hard by, old and curious, and, in fact, all sorts of prints and etchings were sold. This shop was a favourite resort of mine, and I soon became intimate with the owner, and derived much useful information from him on the subject of engraving and engravers in general. His stock included books on the subject of the fine arts, some of a most curious and rare description. Most picture-dealers and collectors knew this print-seller, because it often happened that where paintings which had come into their possession had been engraved they were anxious to acquire such engravings, in order to add interest and enhance the value of the original works. When my acquaintance with the print-seller had ripened into friendship, he proposed that I should rent his third-floor back room, to which I readily assented. The house was old, but spacious, having evidently been once occupied by people of consequence, before it was converted into a shop. My landlord occupied the basement floor, which, beside the print-room, included a small triangular-shaped back parlour, which looked into a court. In this room he took his meals, smoked, and slept, in a lonely, snug sort of way; for though, like myself, he had no relations to comfort or annoy him—being a downright bookworm—the dreariest of winter nights seemed to him not too long. By his advice I bought a straw mattrass, which could be rolled up and placed in a convenient closet during the day, and I was thus enabled to receive a patron, if one chanced to appear, without betraying the extremely limited resources of my establishment. If my friend was better off than myself, he never showed it by his mode of life, which was economical in all things. Following his example, I lived on a mere trifle. A near market supplied little dainties for next to nothing, and our evening meals were, considering all things, both varied and sumptuous. Were it to the purpose, I might say something on the subject of marketing for a supper in London. If my friend had not hoarded up gold, he certainly possessed a stock in trade which represented no inconsiderable fortune. He had stored up choice copies of works which I have since ascertained were of the scarcest and most precious description, and which, regarded in the light of property, were almost as readily available as Bank of England notes. In the works of Holbein alone he was rich beyond any known collectors. Among others, I particularly remember well the "Dance of Death," "The Picture Alphabet," and the "Panegyric on Folly." Of the first he had copies of twenty editions; of the second a corresponding number; and of the illustrated Erasmus a great many. At certain seasons the print-collector closed his shop, and went about from morning till night in search of these ancient treasures of art, calling at every book-stall and broker's shop. In addition, he kept up an uninterrupted communication with the auctioneers, in order to secure timely information of sales when illustrated books and prints were to be disposed of. To this indefatigable acquaintance I was much indebted in many ways. He not only instructed me in the qualities of prints, but put me into the way of procuring an honest crust at the same time. By his advice I made small copies in oil of striking engravings. These he left for sale with dealers, or, as he made it appear, sold them outright among his connexions; and he often returned at night with a few shillings, received, as he said, on my account, and without which I should often have gone supperless to bed.

CHAPTER XLVII.

CHEATED BY A PICTURE-DEALER.

This plan of selling my paintings altogether failed when the print-selling season kept my friend within doors. Driven to rely on my own resources, I was soon persuaded that it required as much art to sell a picture as to paint it. For nearly a week I walked about the streets with my brown paper parcel, containing copies in oil of popular prints, without meeting with a single purchaser, or any approach to one; and I never could discover the means by which my landlord had disposed of my productions, until an accident made the whole matter clear in a moment. One evening I returned home with my pack. I was quite wearied, wet through, and in no very good humour. In addition to not having effected any sales, I had left the sole of one of my shoes in a back street in Whitechapel, and had been compelled to walk back to Hatton Garden, limping through the mud. It had rained nearly all the six days of my hawking expedition, and I was half convinced that the weather had some influence on my ill luck—that the rain had put the brokers out of temper. In this mood I entered the print-seller's triangular parlour. At the same instant a customer walked into the shop in a great hurry, leaving the print-seller no time to close some slides, which he had fitted up in a closet, from which the door had been removed. One of the slides thus exposed betrayed, placed in careful order, the majority of the little pictures which I had painted, and supposed to have been sold! The kind print-seller had been no more successful than myself, but he had had the goodness to deceive me, in order to spare my feelings. Moreover, he had paid me so liberally, that I had not only lived (in a frugal manner, it is true), but, in addition, had been enabled to buy a tolerable suit of clothes, and still retain a few shillings in my pocket. I said nothing of my discovery, but, having rectified the accident to my shoe, set out on the following day to solicit work as a picture-restorer. The Jew was gone on a trip to the continent, and his establishment was well-nigh closed, so that for several weeks to come I could look for nothing from that quarter; and I felt that I ought not to impose any more copies on my patron, in the triangular parlour. If I was unsuccessful in selling pictures, I very speedily found work. Almost the first dealer I asked gave me a job to repair three pictures of no great value. When these were nearly completed, he called at my studio, and brought several others to undergo the same process. He promised me liberal payment, admired my skill, and said so many flattering things that I began to think I should be able to get a connexion of my own, and work at home on better terms than I got from Lame Lazarus, during the picture season. Since seeing my unsold works in the slide, I had been less frequently to supper in the odd-shaped parlour. My pride had received a check. I had enjoyed my meals while I believed that they were the produce of my own toil, but the fried fish lost its flavour from the time that I found that another had paid for it. In all probability, my landlord guessed the cause of my absence from his fireside.

One morning, when I had just varnished the second lot of paintings which the dealer had left with me to renovate, the print-seller entered my studio on the third floor, a very unusual thing with him, as he was not fond of climbing three pairs of stairs, without an object in view. I was just congratulating myself on having completed my contract. As soon as the varnish was dry, I should take home the work, and receive enough to pay off all my debts ; the principal one being an arrear of three weeks' rent for the room

I inhabited. "Ah, my kind friend," I exclaimed, as the landlord entered, "I shall have the pleasure of paying you to-morrow at the latest. See here, I have completed my task."

"You have but a poor opinion of me," he replied, "if you imagine that the trifle you owe me is the cause of my present visit."

"I do believe it is not," I answered; "but that is no reason why I should not pay you."

"You need not distress yourself on that account," said the collector of prints. "I will not deprive you of your little gains. The cash you are to receive may be useful to you in many ways, and I would rather, if you have no objections, wait for my rent, or, if you will allow me, I would take one or two of your little copies in payment, instead of cash."

"You shall do nothing of the kind," I hastened to say. "My little pictures are rubbish which nobody besides yourself will so much as look at. You shall have no more of them, and those which you have I will take off your hands sooner or later."

My kind friend looked distressed at these words, and was about to reply, when the picture-dealer for whom I had been working entered the room and prevented further explanation.

The dealer appeared delighted, and no doubt was so, to find the restoration complete and ready to his hand, and pronounced the workmanship to be excellent. He asked if I thought the varnish sufficiently dry to allow of the pictures being removed, and, without waiting for a reply, proceeded to put them face to face, securing a small space between them by means of bits of cork at the corners, and, this done, he pinned them in a cloth, very neatly, observing as he did so, that I was the most punctual picture-renovator he had ever found, and the most careful one too. "In proof of how highly I value your skill," said he, "I have brought you a portrait of my poor father, who was, like yourself, a distinguished artist. You will perceive," he continued, placing the portrait in a good light on the easel, "if you examine the eyes very closely, that some mischievous villain has destroyed the pupils with a pin." I looked and found the eyes as he described them, and he went on, "I want you to take the smallest pencil you have, and use the utmost skill you can command, and in a happy moment, when your hand is quite steady, repair these injuries."

I offered to do as he wished in his presence, in order, as I told him, that he might not be necessitated to lose sight of a relic which he so much valued. This he objected to, on the score of the agitation which he felt, and which he was afraid, he said, he might communicate to me. He would prefer that I should touch the picture alone, and, when I had satisfied myself, I should carry it to his house, with my account of what he owed me, and receive payment for the whole.

With this arrangement, which I confess was not quite to my satisfaction, he put his parcel of the three paintings under his arm, took an affectionate glance at his father's portrait, and left the studio, apparently wiping away a tear.

The two specks in the eyes referred to occupied me about two minutes, and, having touched them, I ran down-stairs to finish the conversation with my landlord, which had been suddenly interrupted. I told him how pleased I was with my success, and about the portrait, and the injury it had received, and of the affectionate regard with which the dealer had viewed it. My friend said little, but I fancied that he did not feel quite at his ease. In the evening, according to the minute directions I had received, I took the portrait to the dealer's shop, and found it empty: and the words "to let" very conspicuously daubed on the window. I did not on the instant lose heart, for I concluded that it would be easy to find him whom I sought, while I held possession of an object so dear to him—and walked leisurely down the street with the intention of making inquiries. I had not proceeded many yards when I was accosted by another picture-merchant, who was smoking his pipe at his shop door. "What have you got there?" he asked. I showed him the portrait, and inquired if he knew where so-and-so had removed to. He answered that he did not know, and did not care—that it was no matter where, provided it was at a considerable distance, as so-and-so was a doubtful party. Hearing these words I grew alarmed, and told the merchant my story from beginning to end, whereupon he burst into a loud laugh, and told me that I had been cheated, that the story of the portrait was a well-known invention, and the portrait itself was no more the likeness of the knave's father than it was his: that the story of the portrait was a stale trick that he had played on a former occasion with a pretended portrait of his mother, a worthless picture like the one in my hand, and of less value than the canvas on which it was painted.

The whole matter now appeared clear to my comprehension. I had indeed been most wofully cheated out of a week's earnings. For the first time since my residence in the metropolis, I found myself hungry, penniless, and in debt.

CHAPTER XLVIII.

BECOME A LIGHT PORTER.

In spite of my resolution to the contrary, I was compelled to permit my friend, the print-seller, to take more of my little copies in payment for rent, and to provide necessary food; but I felt so strongly that he took them rather out of kindness than because he wanted them, though he good-naturedly asserted the contrary, that I made him promise to allow me to redeem them when prosperity occurred to me. Meanwhile I hung about the Jew's door, in Hatton Garden, in order to be in the way in case anything turned up. After a few weeks, Lame Lazarus appeared on the scene with more than ordinary ill-temper pictured in his ill-favoured face. He would scarcely notice those who had anticipated his arrival with hopes of employment. "There was nothing doing," he said, "and every promise of a bad season. People were failing everywhere: he had lost a fortune by this man, and another fortune by that man, and, in fact, he was ruined to all intents and purposes." Such was his daily cry, and I believe that he actually did lose some fifty pounds by a barrister of Gray's Inn about this time. One morning I took my stand in the door-way, at the usual time, waiting to learn if anything had come in, when I observed the place in great confusion, and all the workpeople, carvers, gilders, and china-menders passing in and out of the warehouse, laden with furniture and ornaments, which the Jew had housed for a long time for a gentleman who had been absent on the continent. I had been thinking of turning my hand to anything rather than be beholden to any one, and here an opportunity offered. The Jew seemed to guess my thoughts, and bade me follow the example of the others, which I willingly did, and sallied forth in the direction of Bloomsbury, carrying on my head an arm-chair of the Elizabethan pattern. I managed my first load tolerably well, because I was enabled to set it down many times by the way, and take a few minutes' rest in it. Unhappily for me, Lame Lazarus caught sight of me thus comfortably seated, and, with his usual amiable disposition, contrived that my next load should be of a less convenient kind. In fact, he, with great effort, placed a figure in bronze, an Atlas carrying the globe, on my unfortunate shoulders. I staggered from the first, but would not complain. Determined to do anything in the way of honest employment, I made a desperate effort and crossed the road. The Jew amused himself by remarking that, "whereas, Atlas carried the world, I carried the world and Atlas into the bargain." My load seemed but a trifle, for the figure was not more than twenty inches in height; being, however, of solid metal, its weight was considerable, and the difficulty was increased by the fact that I could not set it down to rest, as I could the chair. I had not proceeded far up Holborn Hill, and was only just opposite the Black Bull, when my foot caught in a broken pavement, and I stumbled. It was beyond my power to recover my balance. Atlas was too much for me, and, falling backward, the bronze came down with a dull, heavy thud, and the globe, which formed so striking a feature in the work of art, got loosened by the fall, and went rolling down the hill at a rapid pace. I should have fallen myself, but for a friendly hand. Signor Altoviti, in company with the owner of the bronze, happened to be passing at the moment, and saved me from measuring my length upon the earth. The gentleman seemed amused at my mishap, and the Signor particularly so; but I soon discovered that their merriment was not at my expense, but at the Jew's, who, following behind, had witnessed the descent of the figure, and was observed in full pursuit of the rolling globe, as it made its hasty way toward Farringdon Street, where it came to a pause, and was captured. Signor Altoviti lost no time in representing on the wall of his studio the exciting incident of the Jew in full chase of the globe, which brought the matter to a pleasant termination to all but myself, for it transpired that my foot was sprained in such a manner that I was confined to the house for a week.

This was the first time I had been absolutely helpless and dispirited. Hitherto I had imparted to no one my interest in Signor Bezza's daughter. The Jew alone knew of my attachment to Laura, and to him the affair was of the minutest concern. Every day, however, drew me nearer to the print-seller, whose kindness was irresistible. To him I told my story, and found a friendly hearer. This led to his narrating to me his curious experiences as a print-collector.

He had commenced life at twelve years of age with a shilling's worth of ballads, which he used to display on an awning, inclosing a piece of waste ground in the Commercial Road. From ballads he went into the picture business, his stock consisting of coloured engravings of "Balaam and his Ass," the "Prodigal Son," and subjects of a like description spread out in an old umbrella. From the streets and by-ways he had aspired to a stall, from a stall to a shop, and so on, until he had become a respectable shopkeeper and celebrated as an authority in the trade and among connoisseurs in general. He had read much on the subject of his calling, and had a wonderful memory. He recognised at a glance the precise condition of an impression, and had at his tongue's end an appropriate word to describe that condition. He taught me the technicalities of the craft. He kept a back kitchen for a work-room, where he bleached and mounted his prints, and, being, like Signor Altoviti, entirely free from jealousy of rivals, he permitted me to watch and learn the process of bleaching and mounting, and thus added to my stock of experience in art matters. The print-seller had an interesting face. His forehead was broad and full: his eyes large and bright, and his complexion fair and transparent. A moustache helped to hide, but did not wholly conceal, a blemish in the mouth. The lower jaw was what is termed underhung, denoting a certain coarseness of instinct, so that one was not a little surprised to find in him a pattern of modesty, a fact which I traced to the absorbing influence of his pursuit after objects of interest and refinement. Leisure he might be said never to have had, and, therefore whatever evil tendencies nature might have implanted in him, no opportunities had been given them for their display. One of his great virtues was an indescribable fondness for children, on whom he doted to a degree unusual. To the tiny toddlers about his house he became almost indispensable. He dried their tears, he gave them all his waste prints, he kept heaps of copper money to dispense among them, and bought cargoes of fruit, toys, and every conceivable thing which a child might covet. Of course he was a general favourite among the juveniles. Yet he was as melancholy a wight as ever lived. His mind, however, was elastic, and he could be witty, droll, sarcastic, and humane, all in perfection. Rare thoughts and a thousand beauties of expression fell from him in those moments, when pale Melancholy, as if out of pure compassion, had left him. In an unhappy hour and through a fatal mistake he had fallen in love. At the time of my making his acquaintance he was in his forty-first year, and grey hairs had begun to mingle their silvery freshness with the brown. His was an odd love affair for such a time of life. He told me of it with a frank simplicity I despair of imitating.

CHAPTER XLIX.

THE PRINT-SELLER'S STORY.

The night on which my landlord told me his story I had observed him to be in a very unusual mood. When not stirring the fire he was puffing his tobacco at a great pace, as if, like the oracles of old, he sought to enshroud himself in mystery, before delivering himself of some weightier matters than ordinary. But, however he might hide himself from the eye, a quick ear could detect in his voice a something new and strange, as he proceeded with his account of the only love adventure he had gone through in all his life. The case had its peculiarities.

At the corner of a near street was an old-fashioned eating-house, where each day, Sundays excepted, the window steamed with legs of roast pork, fillets of veal, and huge rounds of boiled beef garnished with carrots and supported by suet puddings. This shop had been kept by a very plain, honest old lady for a great many years. The print-seller found it convenient, and it had been his custom to dine and sup there each day and night with equal regularity, until an acquaintance sprang up and he became a privileged person in the establishment: and instead of sitting with the other customers, he was permitted to take his food in the small back parlour shut off from the common dining-room by a screen and red curtain—a very snug corner where exactly four persons would sit and enjoy the pleasures of privacy in the very midst, as it were, of the busy throng. Things had gone on in this pleasant way for seven years or more—the print-seller and the honest landlady becoming more and more familiar, until each consulted the other on every subject of the least consequence. The excellent landlady almost considered the customer in the light of a brother, and felt bound to take care of and advise him on all social matters. And it often happened that a chance word dropped by a customer within hearing, or a report of some circumstance in the papers, or a story read from one of the score-and-half of amusing books that formed the coffee-room library, would give rise to discussions on the interesting theme of matrimony: and the suggestive proprietress never allowed a day to pass without advising the print-seller to adopt that state. All she could say, however, on that subject never made the least impression on the collector of prints.

At length it became his turn to tender advice, and impart words of comfort. The hostess had heard of the sudden death in the country of an only brother, for whom she had more than ordinary affection. Her daily guest knew by report all the particulars of this brother and his family affairs, so that when the news of the good man's death reached the mistress of the dining-room he had his share of the common sorrow. There were the shutters, at least three out of six, to be left up: there was the mourning to make, and a journey to prepare for, for the landlady did not hesitate about the absolute propriety of attending her brother's funeral, and, what was more than all, of taking charge of an orphan daughter, an only child, now left with the neighbours. The brother had long been a widower. The print-seller said and did all in his power to render the calamity as light as possible. A night was spent in arranging plans for the comfort of the orphan, who was henceforth to form one of the inmates of the bar-parlour.

"I expect we shall soon spoil her between us," said the landlady.

"Poor child!" exclaimed the print-seller, whose pity was at once awakened on behalf of the country maiden.

In little more than a week, the night coach made its appearance at an early hour at the Black Bull, on Holborn Hill, and found the print-seller in waiting: and as the aunt had in the course of a long journey talked very much to her niece about her favourite daily guest, that young lady was fully prepared to treat him as a friend almost before she saw him: and he, in like manner, when he beheld the stranger step from the coach, with her pale face and large eyes so full of sorrow, at once made up his mind to love her; but in what character he did not attempt to decide, and hardly dared to think. He had expected to meet a mere child, and he found a young woman of some eighteen years of age, and beautiful beyond description. A few days seemed to put matters in order. The niece proved quite an able assistant to the aunt, and in the hurry of business her grief became in some degree modified; new scenes and new activity alleviating the sadness of her great bereavement. The regular customers showed her great respect, while some of the juniors envied the print-seller his superior privileges as bar-parlour guest. Yet he deserved all the happiness which the society and conversation of the new comer could afford him: for he did everything he could to make her forget her sorrows, or rather to reconcile her to the loss of parents on whom she had doted. He himself had been left an orphan in the first year of his life. He told her so, and she sighed and looked at him with pitying looks. He stifled the feeling which took possession of his breast. He tried to appear indifferent; and in order not to indulge in tender personal reminiscences, flew to ordinary topics, such as theatres, public buildings, and more especially the grand churches of the metropolis —and went with Jessy (for that was the young lady's name) and her aunt to St. Paul's and Westminster Abbey, and one or other church, every succeeding Sunday. In the natural kindness of his heart, he devised other attentions. Out of the vast stores of prints which he possessed, he made a handsome album, containing views of countries, and costumes of all nations, and many other subjects, and had it bound in morocco at considerable expense. Being possessed of much information of a popular kind, he directed his conversation to explanations of the pictures, and thus in the most agreeable manner he combined instruction with amusement. Not to flatter the pupil, she stood in need of some such tutor, for while nature had done so much for her, art had been entirely idle: and beyond the ordinary matters of farm life and village gossip, she had but few ideas. But if Jessy was ignorant, she had a ready way of seizing on the pretty histories which the print-seller repeated to her—or which she found in the quaint volumes left for her perusal: and with equal readiness did she appreciate the kind intentions of her friend and instructor, and, in her own modest, charming and simple way, repay his kindness by looks more eloquent than words, and by words more expressive than any which the books she read contained: at least, so thought the infatuated seller of engravings.

This intimacy between the solitary man and the unsophisticated girl increased day by day, and yet it was long before particular notice was taken of its extent and importance by those concerned. Jessy was no sooner out of mourning than she might be seen walking beneath the dome of St. Paul's, wearing a tasteful and costly shawl which her aunt's guest had presented to her on her nineteenth birthday, and the little hand which hid itself beneath that shawl clasped a tiny prayer-book of a most rare order, which even a duchess might have carried. This also came from the courtly presenter of the shawl. Flowers of the sweetest fragrance, early violets, and primroses, were frequently seen in the little parlour: the print-seller was ever an early visitor at Covent Garden when flowers were in season. All this was very charming, because no harm was thought or intended. But where was it all to end? A year passed by, and the sympathetic, grave man saw only grace and sweetness in the orphan who had come to drive away the evil spirits that had vexed his heart so long. Dreary languor no longer oppressed him and filled his house with grim and shadowy forms. The days were long when he saw not Jessy. The moments flew by when he sat by her side in the little parlour, which was nightly. All traces of grief had now left Jessy's face. When evening came she reached out her books and trinkets to gaze upon them for the hundredth time. All this while no explanation was either asked or desired, or felt to be necessary. At length the customers took the delicate subject up, and at the remoter tables the print-seller and his attentions to the niece became the usual topic of conversation among the workmen of a type-foundry hard by. The men all agreed that the attentive print-seller was all that could be desired, saving that he was a trifle too advanced in years. On the latter point there could be no manner of doubt. One of the observers took upon himself to favour the mistress of the establishment with his opinion on the subject. The good woman was several days before the man's meaning came into her head, and, when she did come to understand to what the mechanic's remarks referred, she laughed "till she was ready to drop,"—so absurd seemed the idea to her in her simplicity. "You need not seem so astonished," observed the officious mechanic, "for I could name half a dozen instances in which older men, artists, doctors, and barristers, have persuaded young girls with large fortunes to marry them."

Let it not be supposed that the print-seller himself was innocent of all thoughts on this subject of conversation in the coffee-room. On the contrary, he spent hours, during which he should have slept, in debating the question over and over again. He knew not what to do. He was too far removed from a conceited coxcomb to think for a moment that he was all that a young and beautiful girl could hope for in a husband. But how should he act? He was in a dilemma. Withdraw himself by degrees, said reason and prudence. He began to do so. The first week of this resolve he missed dining with Jessy once. What was the consequence? He had to stay an hour later at night to make up for his mid-day neglect. He made many attempts in this way, and as often failed. The moments were counted; and had he stayed from the bar-parlour one entire day, there would have been little peace in the house.

The customers, who had little else there to engage their attention, made the interesting couple their sole study, and, clever as they were, they were all deceived in the conclusion at which they arrived, which was that the print-seller wanted to break the engagement, that Jessy would not permit him to do so, and that he was an idiot to refuse so beautiful a creature for a wife: and that if she preferred a husband so much older than herself, why, that was her affair, not his. The result was that the poor print-seller, as he reflected upon the matter from his own point of sight, found himself once more given over to sad, perplexing thoughts and serious doubts. He clearly could not reduce the number of his days, but he would try to feel jocund and cheerful: he would by comforts, nay, even by luxuries, do much to make his home a happy one. Perhaps he reflected broadly on the theme of unequal marriages. This life is full of difficulties at every step. How many stumble for lack of experience which only years can give: and were it not wise, therefore, for a young and inexperienced girl like Jessy, for instance, to look up to one ripe in years and wealthy in experience, rather than risk her precious life in the keeping of one as young and as little acquainted with real life as herself? But love, passion, reason, and prudence are seldom united. His reflections did not satisfy himself. They seemed suggested by selfishness, a feeling which found little favour in his eyes. What was he to do? That Jessy evidently loved him to distraction was commonly believed in the room. Her mature suitor was compelled to believe so himself. Again, what was he to do? He took to novel reading, and lighted on some German works which had for their subject the very state of mind in which he found himself. What will Germans not do? Those German writers made it appear that unequal marriages were greatly to be preferred: and, so far from wondering that blooming maidens gave the preference to their seniors, they wondered how any girls of sense and refinement could for a moment permit themselves to be deluded by the auburn locks and thoughtless levity of mere boys. The print-seller read these stories, but failed to be convinced by them. He had too much modesty to lay these highly-coloured novels in the way of Jessy, and when he tried to broach the subject in his own way he failed to make himself understood. His perplexities became greater than ever: for he reflected that, if by abandoning Jessy, whom he loved to distraction, he might never know a moment's happiness again; and at the same time the girl whom he loved, and who undoubtedly loved him, would equally become unhappy, then his imaginary devotion to duty would really be a desertion, a folly, or a crime. He decided that he would make up his mind and at once propose and marry Jessy. With this resolve he collected his scattered property, did up his house to make it worthy of its new occupant, and by degrees fortified himself to bear the brunt of all those meddling reflections and comments which no doubt might, and in all probability would, be made upon his wedding-day.

When everything was complete, his resolve fixed, and his heart involved beyond redemption, he accidentally discovered that Jessy had never loved, never dreamed of loving him, in any other light than as she had loved her own dear parent. He had decided to speak to her on the Friday, but, happening to go suddenly into supper on the previous night, he found cause to lay aside his intentions. He had entered the dining-room, after it was closed to ordinary patrons, and shut the door, when he overheard her on whom he doted speaking in a most feeling and somewhat excited manner. The last words of Jessy fell upon his astonished ear. "I know," she cried, "that I ought to be happy and thankful too, for if heaven took from me father and mother, and left me an orphan, God gave me another mother in you, my dear aunt, and a father in my dear Mr. Dexter;" saying which, and overcome by her filial emotions, she threw her arms round the print-seller's neck, and kissed him for the first time during all the period of their acquaintance.

I asked the print-seller what became of Jessy, as he concluded his narrative, when he informed me that the fat wife of the fat baker next door was the same person; that she was perfectly happy, and that she had never surmised that he, the print-seller, had ever loved her save in the light of a father.

CHAPTER L.

THE POET.

Among the people who came to look over the print-seller's folios was a tall, thin man, who, on the strength of having made a couple of tolerable ballads in his youth, or rather in his boyhood, had gone on song-making all his life, and so beggared himself. This individual had very fine eyes, of which he was so vain that, though past sixty years of age, he used to practise languishing airs before his looking-glass, and persuade himself that he had a way of his own perfectly irresistible. He was, to use his own words, a reverent admirer of the old painters, and talked much of "Guido's divine airs," of "Raphael's killing sweetness," and "Correggio's melting tenderness." When he could scrape together a few pounds, instead of paying vulgar tradesmen, he would speculate on an old picture. It was his practice day by day to poke about in dirty brokers shops in search of hidden gems; and in order that he should not be disappointed, the dealers would hide their daubs where he was likely to hunt. Thus one day our poetical searcher found what he called a "Carlo Dolci" in a coal shed, and on another occasion a "Francesca Mola" in a cellar among old iron-work. After, in this way, securing his gem, he would go straight to the print-seller's to see if it had been engraved, and so hunt among the folios and talk a tiresome amount of nonsense.

The print-seller, as I have said, was a kind man, and knew not how to refuse. Out of gratitude to my host, I made a point of attending to the poet, and by this means we became acquainted. It said something for my constitution and disposition that I was able to endure him. There was no stopping his tongue, no putting him off. When I was ready to drop with fatigue he had the impression that I was in ecstasies with the beauty of his language, and when I looked imploringly up into his face he fancied I was admiring his eyes.

One day, in order further to relieve the master of the shop of his enemy the poet, I took him up to my studio, where he soon made himself at home, sometimes bringing me his presumed old masters for me to operate upon. He was delighted with me, and promised to do for me what he had failed to do for himself, namely, make my fortune. He pronounced me a genius of the highest order, and behaved in all respects like a prince, saving only that he paid me in words instead of coin. After a while, he expressed a wish that I should occupy chambers in his house, as he called it, and, as I was honourably desirous of leaving the print-seller's, I accepted the proposal and moved. I was anxious to leave the print-seller on any pretext, because I foresaw that the longer I remained with him the deeper I should become indebted to him, for his generosity was inexhaustible. I felt ashamed of imposing upon him. Up to this time I had managed, by strict frugality, to keep solvent, but this had been done by some of my prints and books changing hands. I had caused Madame Mitchel to send those up deposited with her on my leaving home in pursuit of the Bezzas. The print-seller, appreciating my feelings, accepted the choicest specimens of books and prints, as security for so much rent due; and I took up my abode with the poet in a large, gloomy house, in the neighbourhood of the Garrick Club, Covent Garden, with a view to restore his "collection of paintings."

At intervals my metrical patron was a most sensible man, and bargained in a business-like way to find me food, and give me five shillings a day for my services. A large empty chamber, immediately over his rooms, I engaged for five shillings a week, as a sleeping apartment, and he chose that I should manipulate on the pictures in his own rooms, where he could watch the progress of renovation. The poet's wife was a very homely sort of woman, very little younger than himself, and unfortunately for her, like him, not overburdened with practical sense. From her I learned the nature of the poet's ordinary occupation. Being an excellent classical scholar, he was employed in one of the chief printing-offices as reader, and he might have lived handsomely on the fruits of his attainments, but for his versifying and picture-collecting, which had been the cause of his being driven from various lodging-houses, from his lack of means to pay his way in the world. For some time the poet's table was well supplied, and hardly a day passed without some fresh luxury of the season being sent in. His employment was irregular, and often left him leisure, and he would stay within doors for whole days, sitting at my back or reclining upon a sofa, talking about the old masters without intermission. Speaking of his verses, he informed me that he seldom composed by day, that inspiration commonly seized him about midnight, and that his happier rhymes were commonly committed to paper by the light of the lamp. This appeared to be true, for one morning, according to custom, on descending into his sitting-room, which had been turned into a studio, I found that, notwithstanding that the sun had risen some two or three hours, the room, contrary to custom, was still in total darkness. I went straight to unbar the shutters, and, having let in the light, I was not a little surprised to behold the gaunt poet in his night-shirt, standing against the table (on which stood an expiring lamp), pen in hand, apparently in a dream. I was too startled to move or speak for the moment, but, recovering myself, I accosted him, when he placed his finger to his lip, as if to enjoin silence; and thus he remained buried in thought—inspiration he called it. At length the pen came into requisition, and for a short period was actively employed, and apparently to my employer's entire satisfaction; for when he ceased writing he snatched up the paper, and eyed it with an unmistakable expression of rapture. I was curious to know what subject had engaged him so earnestly, and ventured to ask him, when, to my utter amazement, he turned, and in a strange, solemn voice, answered, "Laura Bezza," and then, with a couple of strides, passed like an apparition into the adjoining room to complete his interrupted slumbers.

Had I been disposed to make a confidant of the poet he was always so much absorbed in his songs and pictures, and talked so incessantly, that he left me no opportunity; hence my amazement on my hearing him pronounce the name of one whose image was ever in my memory. I could hardly resist following him to ask what he knew of Laura. I conjectured many things, but only the more to feel the whole a mystery.

Possibly the Bezzas were known to my eccentric employer. I determined to ask him for an explanation, the moment that he made his appearance. When he did return, he bore a picture in his hand on which I had been engaged the day before. It was the portrait of a young girl, which by a stretch of fancy I had made to look somewhat like Laura. The poet placed it on the easel, and, unfolding a paper, proceeded to read the verses he had produced, and on which he was employed when disturbed by my intrusion. He read the title, "Laura Bezza," and then the rhymes. They were the most silly I had ever heard. "But the title—how did you come by the title, sir?" I asked, with manifest interest. He pointed to the portrait—the whole matter was explained. While in a fit of abstraction, I had inadvertently written "Laura Bezza" on the panel, and forgotten to remove it. The poet had taken a fancy to the name, and thereupon composed a song about Venice, and gondoliers, marble palaces, and dancing waves, dark eyes, warbling lutes, Georgione and Titian.

CHAPTER LI.

THE LODGING-HOUSE.

ABOUT once in three years, the poet contrived to get so far behind with his landlord, as to make an adjustment of accounts, or change of residence, indispensable, and soon after my engagement began the period for this arrangement came round. His great concern on these occasions, was to secure his manuscripts, and which, on the manifestation of the final danger, he, until he could bring about a settlement, ingeniously stowed away in his hat or umbrella, and conveyed them to a place of greater safety.

The furniture of my sleeping apartment was doomed with the rest, but happily, I had saved sufficient money to buy the mattrass, bed-clothes, one table, and a chair, and with these I began housekeeping on my own account. To this end, also, I engaged the services of a very needy chairwoman, who occupied a cellar at the back of the mansion, which, as I have said, was most spacious. The principal staircase, on which I resided, would admit of three persons ascending it abreast. The balusters were quaintly formed, and the panels ornamented with beautiful scroll-work. I was told that another staircase existed, scarcely less spacious, but of a somewhat plainer character. Each floor consisted of a suite of four rooms. About a dozen families lived under the entire roof, more or less unknown to each other, and, with the exception of my poor charwoman, altogether unknown to myself. I was curious enough to question my attendant about the families on my own floor, and learned that an elderly woman and her daughter lived in the room adjoining, and that a foreign gentleman and his daughter rented three rooms in one part of the house. I was struck by the fact that these foreigners consisted of a gentleman and his daughter, but, as the charwoman described them to be French, I troubled no further about them. My income now was so reduced that, after paying my rent, I had barely means of support, and was compelled to part with the whole of my carving tools, which I had retained for practice, both in wood and stone. I sold them, a few at a time, to the keeper of a second-hand shop, in the neighbourhood. At length, by frequent application among the small brokers, I got to be a little known, and after a few weeks, a dealer gave me an old picture to renovate. This man honestly paid me on the completion of the work, and recommended me to another small trader, like himself: and thus, by degrees, I made a connexion. At intervals I made copies of small prints, and sold them for a few shillings apiece, and now and then, carried a small landscape, or piece of still-life, to an auction mart which did business chiefly in pictures. Often, when no biddings had been made for my productions, the auctioneer, after trying them in two or three successive sales, would bring a bill against me for more than the pictures were worth, as things went. The charwoman who waited upon me evidently entertained no very exalted idea of my resources. All my expedients to veil the real state of things did not succeed with her, and, with the best of intentions, no doubt, she communicated her impressions to the antiquated occupant of the next room, and thus brought about the least endurable of my annoyances. This old woman had a loud bass voice, was of a talkative turn, and so far silly as not always to know what she was talking about. Without paying much attention to her disjointed sentences, I could often make out that the drift of her interminable talk nearly always related to the private affairs of some one known to her, and frequently to people living in the same house. At length my turn came round. She spoke of me as the artist in the next room, or as the poor young man, or the poor gentleman, as her descriptive powers varied. In vain the daughter tried to arrest the mother's garrulity. The old lady's chief concern was, that she had no place, no sitting-room, into which to invite me. She grew more concerned for me day by day. If I was silent, as was my wont, she fancied that I might have died —if I made a noise, that I was taken ill—if I coughed, that I was gone into a consumption. I forbade the charwoman to speak of me, but my injunctions were of no avail. I continued the favourite theme with my near neighbour.

Over the old lady lived a couple of shoemakers, who likewise troubled themselves much with the concerns of their fellow-lodgers. They exerted themselves in the sarcastic line. They had evidently both seen and heard of the painter below. "Poor devil" was one of their remarks. One of them kept company with the daughter of the old lady with the bass voice, and it was through this that I came to know of the style they employed when speaking of me. To do the old lady justice, she was filled with indignation at their insolence. The stoop had not left me, which, as I have previously stated, I at one time acquired, which led these sarcastic cordwainers to say that "my head made its appearance round a corner some ten minutes sooner than the rest of my body." My boots had acquired the infirmity to run down on one side, right and left, which made the rascals to remark that my boots could not agree, and that while one wished to walk up one side the street the other insisted upon going up the opposite side. Something, one day, in the appearance of my garments was made by them an occasion to report a general defect of buttons and recourse to primitive fastenings. On this point the would-be wags observed that I could not dress myself without a ball of string, nor undress without a knife. Touching my attenuated appearance, which a faulty commissariat is apt to engender, the rogues suggested that, in venturing out in the wind, it would be as well if I carried a bag with me, so that in the event of my being blown into bits, which would be pretty sure to be the case, the bag would be useful into which to convey the collected fragments to my friends, that is, if I had any friends.

CHAPTER LII.

THE COBBLER'S PLOT.

In process of time the tones of the old lady's voice became less harsh, which improvement I learned from her repeated assertion was owing to the constant use of stewed onions. It was an advantage to learn indirectly that she frequently employed that relishing article of diet. Day by day new topics of discourse came up in which I and my affairs were more or less a feature of interest. One morning the old lady became more animated then ordinary in my defence against some charge which my enemies above had made against me, as it turned out by way of practical joke; but the particulars of which did not reach my ears, for the daughter was evidently suppressing the mother's voice, from the stifled indistinctness which began to affect the old lady's utterance. The subject had something to do with jealousy and revenge and the tipsy cobbler's wife who lived in the attic.

My gratuitous tormentors had started a report, the direct purport of which I could not glean from the disjointed utterances made in my neighbour's room. The fact is, the visible decay of my means had proceeded so far that I had become the victim of a practical joke.

On the evening following my incidental knowledge of this plot I was sitting musingly over a handful of warm cinders for which I had raked and re-raked the ashes of the grate half a dozen times over. I was sitting with my back partly to the door which led into my room. The sun had set, but the sky still reflected a chilly, dismal glare and lit up my face. I was pondering upon what I should do on the morrow; I had hoped against hope. Laura, alas, I had almost grown afraid to inquire after. My garments had begun to illustrate my fortune; my feet had already excited notice; the very mice had ceased to visit my cupboard. I had gone down lower and lower. Pride had prompted me to conceal, even to deny, my needs to the few who would instantly have served me, until I had no longer the heart to make known my wants. As I still sat by the cheerless grate, for by this time the fire had quite gone out, I was suddenly startled by a loud noise on the stairs. I had barely recovered the shock, when my door was thrown open and a dark form came rushing across the room. I had not attempted to rise, and, in a sort of stupor into which my previous reflections had thrown me, I gazed on the intruder with the same fixed look I had worn while watching the last lingering light in the sky. The man—for the gloom was not so great but one could see that the intruder was a man—stood confronting me, exclaiming in a threatening, husky, excited, inebriated voice, "Where's the painter? Bring a light; I will kill him;" and more to the same effect. Still I moved not, understood not the meaning of this outrage. At last, tired with imprecation, the ruffian laid his hands upon me. In an instant I was aroused. I rushed upon my assailant, and, with a fury and an energy that I knew not that I possessed, I shook him off. By this time the house was in an uproar, for the old lady in the next room had screamed murder at the top of her very effective voice: and a crowd of lodgers came rushing in to learn what was the matter, and, as I thought, to spy out my beggarly condition. Then it was that I discovered who had been my assailant. It was the drunken, jealous cobbler, whom his mischievous friends had thus incited. Drunk as he was when the lights were brought, a glance seemed to suffice to convince him that he had been deceived. "It is a lie; I have been deceived," he exclaimed, as he looked into my face. I returned not his glance and but little heeded his words. My eyes were riveted on the curious assemblage who now filled the apartment; I could not be deceived in two persons who were gazing at me. They were Signor Bezza and Laura.

CHAPTER LIII.

THE ITALIAN'S FIRESIDE.

SIGNOR BEZZA was the first to speak. I rose from my seat as he approached me with open arms and astonishment pictured in his face. He seized me with both hands, and glanced around the room; and again at me. I seemed to read his thoughts in his face. "You, my old friend, whom I have known and loved, living here in penury, and I all the time in the same house living in affluence!" "Here, Laura, come," he exclaimed aloud; "here is our good friend found at last. Neighbours," he added, "I know not to what chance I am indebted for this discovery, but I am happy in having found this gentleman whom I had long lost and mourned. Strange that he should all this time be living under the same roof with me, and I not know it. Passing strange; I have been more than anxious in seeking my friend, because I have in my keeping a sum of money belonging to him, and which, from the reports which have been spread among you, you may well judge, will be more than welcome to him at this time. Neighbours, leave us, I pray you, to settle our little affairs together, and make our mutual explanations. To-morrow, I promise you, will put a very different face upon this matter than at this moment it wears."

These words had the effect for which they were so well calculated. The lodgers retired, and I followed Signor Bezza and Laura to their side of the house, where cheerfulness and plenty prevailed. The room into which I was ushered was even luxuriously furnished, the table sumptuously spread. Fire and lamp lent warmth and light. A sudden change came over me. I felt like one newly risen from the dead, yet with the graveclothes still hanging about him.

The Italian was not only a genius in the art of modelling, he was also too refined a gentleman to see that I was not at ease, or to take the least notice of my garb. One might have sworn that he did not perceive any change in my outward aspect. When once by his fireside, the look of wonder was gone, and all his wonted ease and old manner returned. But what shall I say of Laura? She seemed to have treasured up all the wealth of her affectionate nature into one huge hoard, in order that when she found me she might astonish me by its abundance. Perhaps, had she found me in affluence, I might, in turn, have found her a riddle difficult to read—cold, haughty, distant, reserved; but now her every look proclaimed unconcealed gladness. Her silence, for she said little, was more eloquent than words, for her words would never have told her kind thoughts in half their fulness. Her face, so symmetrical, changed its expression every minute. First there was pleasure for the present, then sorrow for the past, for she had, like her father, comprehended my late history at a glance, and struggled to hide from me her real affliction at the thought of what I might have undergone. For awhile she neglected her father, and made my wants her sole study, and then, remembering, she flew to her parent to make amends for her unintentional inattention.

After dinner the Signor produced a bottle of choice, delicate Italian wine, and some cigarettes of Laura's own making, as he told me. By degrees the night wore on, and the Signor, according to custom, called for his Dante—his never-failing solace; and Laura and I had opportunity to tell our own stories to one another in our own way.

CHAPTER LIV.

EXPLANATIONS AND PROJECTS.

THE morning after my happy discovery of the Italians the Signor presented himself in my dreary apartment, with the express view of talking over the past and the future. He began by assuring me that he had remained awake all night reflecting upon the best course to be taken for the welfare of his child and my happiness. He then astonished me by a piece of information respecting old Lazarus, which was altogether opposed to my experiences of that individual. He assured me that he had been much indebted to the Jew—that it was by his assistance he had made his way to London—that he had received many important commissions from him since, and that in fact old Lazarus had proved a good patron to him. Furthermore, he described the Hebrew as very wealthy, having establishments on the continent, and particularly one at the Hague:

that old Lazarus took a special interest in my welfare, and that it was to him I in some degree stood indebted for a sum of money which had been sent by Madame Mitchel, while on her death-bed, to be equally divided between Laura and myself. In verification of the latter circumstance, the Signor handed me fifty pounds, in the name of Madame Mitchel, and ten pounds, which, as I have stated, I left with that kind landlady when I set out with old Lazarus on my search after the Italians. But scarcely had I time to take heart at this unexpected piece of fortune, when the Signor dissipated my joy by remarking that he was about to leave England and take his daughter with him. He was, he said, acquainted with my unfortunate career in the metropolis, and thought none the worse of me for my want of success; only that he must object to my marriage with Laura, until I should succeed in persuading Fortune to be more kind to me than she had been hitherto. "You English," he observed, "are most thoughtless in often rushing into marriage with little means to support that state when inevitable expenses arise. Single, you do very well; being able to live, so you say, on five shillings a week; but when married, you are ready to confess that five shillings a day is little enough. When I hear people assert, as only English people do assert, that the married is no more expensive than the single state, and that children involve no additional expense—that it takes no more to fill six mouths than two—why, I confess that I am not convinced by what I hear. Anyhow, my mind is made up; Laura will never have my consent to marry any one, save yourself, and she will not have that until you are established in something like a permanent condition of prosperity. Meanwhile, perhaps it is desirable that we part. Of your success, of which I have now no doubt, I shall hear through our friend Lazarus, who, as I have said, has your interest at heart, as he has long had mine."

At these words of the Signor's I was speechless, and knew not what to say, for I had not thought to part from Laura in this manner, and so suddenly too. The Signor of course guessed my thoughts, for he could not fail to perceive the effect the determination he had announced had upon me.

"You have one fault," he proceeded; "you are proud beyond measure; in proof of which, I may instance your having immured yourself in the way that you have, when all the time you had friends like the good print-seller, who is every inch a gentleman, and who would have known how to serve you in a way you could have permitted. Then there was my friend Altoviti, who would have opened his large heart, had he known of your necessities. For my friend Lazarus, perhaps, I cannot say quite so much; but of this I am sure, that the harshness he displayed was in part put on to try your patience and endurance, to which qualities in any man he will in the end bow down."

I was about to reply to this last remark of Signor Bezza's touching my want of patience and endurance, when he cut me short, saying that the Jew had had proof in abundance that I was not deficient in these respects, and, but for the untoward incident which separated me from the Hebrew, I should have had evidence of what Bezza had asserted, as to the interest which old Lazarus had in my welfare.

"But you will permit me to see Laura again before we part?" I asked.

"It is impossible. I have already removed her from this house, where I have lingered but too long. I have commissions abroad which may not be neglected. Go, replenish yourself with dress and tools. Call on old Lazarus. You owe him thanks, and, if I mistake not, he will be most glad to see you, although he may not discover the state of his feelings. He and I have arranged an engagement for you, which will gratify you, he having held back a commission which it rests with you to make remunerative. It is in the way of picture estoration. The work is ready, it has only waited," he added with that encouraging flattery an Italian can so gracefully employ, "a Robert Dalby to do it. Addio! you have my blessing, you have my love—you have Laura's. Take my advice, and all will end well; and, according to your greatest bard, 'All's well that ends well.'"

CHAPTER LV.

A FORTUNATE COMMISSION.

Some days after the interview I had with Signor Bezza I was on my way, in company with old Lazarus, to the residence of a gentleman of great wealth, an ex-governor and West Indian planter. The object of our visit was made known to me as we went along. The ex-governor had made more money than he knew what to do with, was filling his house with paintings of all kinds, and wanted some one to put them in order. The Jew, being aware of this, had considerately recommended me for the task. So far the Signor's words were verified, and Lazarus had, indeed, rendered me a service unasked.

The mansion was situated in a retired corner of a park, some three miles out of town. The grounds had in part been replanted by their present wealthy owner, who, feeling that he had not many years to live, had transplanted trees, already arrived at maturity, and with an eye to the present and the picturesque, had in a few years produced the effects of a century's growth. He had thrown up embankments and covered them with underwood, imparting to the scene all the charms of wildness and disorder. Immediately in front of the house, on the contrary, all that was fair and smooth met the eye. A small lake, clear as a mirror, reflected gay parterres and lawns and level walks: while in adjoining meadows water-fowls abounded, lending animation to a pleasant stream; and ponds, well margined with flags and rushes, afforded refuge for carp and tench. The interior of the mansion was in keeping with the grounds around. Shrubs and flowers filled every spare nook, and, ranged about upon the tesselated pavement of the hall, they mingled their variegated foliage with graceful sculptured forms.

The principal personage at this enchanting residence, next to the proprietor, was an aged brother, who came forth to meet us at the porch. Our arrival had been duly announced by Sambo, a woolly-headed porter, who salaamed in his best manner, on receiving our names. The brother led us into the presence of the owner, who received us with Oriental breeding. We were invited to partake of refreshment, which numerous servants supplied with noiseless attentions. Our wealthy host barely noticed the repast, except to press some particular dish upon my notice, excusing his own want of appetite by saying that at my years he could eat a whole sheep. The Jew needed no pressing, and talked very animatedly when he had partaken of a little wine. I learned from passing remarks that Signor Bezza had often been a guest in the same house, and that old Lazarus had imparted to the ex-governor some particulars of my life. I was wise enough to leave to my Hebrew friend the task of making terms for me, feeling sure that he knew better than myself the value of services which he had had so many opportunities of appraising. The result far exceeded my anticipations; and with one of those sanguine transitions of feeling, which only the young, familiar with vicissitudes make, I already fancied myself a rich man.

On our way back, the Jew did not forget to congratulate me on my good fortune, without, however, taking any credit to himself, as he well might have done, for his part in the business. I did not fail, however, to express my obligations for the unexpected service he had done me. "At the table of this retired Indian planter," Lazarus observed, "you will meet with scores of wealthy collectors of art-relics, and a connexion valuable to you will be made in time. Altoviti assures me that you are well versed in the principles of art. He says he would trust you with the restoration of a Raphael. I ought to have kept you to myself," added the Jew, with a touch of his natural manner.

Nothing could be pleasanter than the execution of my engagement, to renovate the wealthy planter's pictures. The consciousness of gain, and the allurements of its consequences on my prospects, made the time pass rapidly, which otherwise might have appeared long. At length my work over, old Lazarus startled and interested me, by proposing that I should accompany him on a journey of business, to Holland. Was my mysterious friend about to discover to me some of his business connexions, or show me his importance in some way? I could not understand it. However, Holland was a country full of interest for me, in connection with art; but I confess that I was chiefly attracted by the hope of joining the Bezzas, for the Jew had more than once hinted that Laura and her father had, to use an expression of the Jew's, "favoured that country with their presence."

CHAPTER LVI.

A JOURNEY TO HOLLAND.

GREAT was my joy when, after many delays, on one rainy morning in November, I and my friendly tormentor took passage for Rotterdam. My travelling companion had a different costume for every class of business in which he engaged. When selling, he looked very grand with jewellery; when buying, he appeared poverty-stricken and chapfallen. On setting out for Holland, he presented himself in a shabby suit of fustian; and carried over his shoulder a sack; he was to all appearance, the poorest person on board the vessel. To be in keeping with his forlorn aspect, we took deck passages, in common with a large number of German drovers, who had brought cattle to England, and were then on their way home. Little thought that motley array of passengers that my shabby acquaintance carried about him wealth enough to buy the vessel in which we were embarked. Yet such was the fact.

Unaccustomed to sea life, it was not long before I lay prostrate upon a heap of chain and rope, near the middle of the deck, whence, when night set in, the captain kindly ordered me to be carried below. I had sufficient consciousness remaining to buy some brandy of the steward, which so far restored my strength that I began to look about me, by the light of a dimly-burning lamp, when the first object that met my gaze was the Jew, crouched down in the corner like a dog. His proper place, of course, was like mine, upon deck; but, disliking salt water, he had slunk down unperceived, to the snug place where I beheld him. I was about to call out to him, when he enjoined silence; he had no wish to pay four shillings fare in addition to what he had paid. It was a rainy, boisterous night, so much so, that the captain's heart was moved for the poor drovers, and he permitted them, also, to descend for shelter. They came below half drowned. There was only standing room, and, as they all smoked enormous pipes, the place became suffocating. What with the odour of their vile tobacco, and greasy steaming garments, I began to wish that the good captain had allowed me to perish on deck, or that he had thrown me overboard. And yet amid the smother and confusion (they all appeared to be dancing), I could now and then see old Lazarus tempting the poor fellows with his trinkets. He came to my side as if to comfort me, but altered his mind and drank the little brandy I had left: he had to loosen my fingers one by one to get it from my miserable clutch. In return for this untimely freedom, he stooped down and whispered in my ear that I should soon behold the Signor and Laura, rightly calculating that this piece of news would obliterate all thought of the little transaction from which I had just suffered. The Jew had the art of making, even the facts of his ordinary knowledge bring him in something.

Morning, which seemed as though it would never come, arrived at last, and found us in sight of land. Smooth water announced our entrance into the broad river, when I went up on deck, not much refreshed, but very hungry, after that terrible night in the hold. In the course of the morning I ordered some coffee for my breakfast. The Jew expressed his amazement at so great a piece of extravagance on my part, and, in order not to lay himself open to the charge of inconsistency, he partook of my loaf and coffee, and forgot to pay his part of the reckoning, which was very characteristic of him, and, as it appeared to me then, quite of a piece with his character all through. Arriving at a shallow part of the river, we had the misfortune to run aground:

whereupon the captain made the following announcement:—"We shall stay where we are, gentlemen, for about fourteen hours. Those who happen to be in a hurry, can land here and walk to Dort, whence they can go in a barge to Rotterdam. That's all I have to say."

Strange enough, old Lazarus was the only individual who chose to land. He had made arrangements to sup in Rotterdam that night, and punctuality was one of his virtues.

A miserable-looking wretch, who had by means of stakes, hurdles, stones, and faggots, rescued a strip of land from the river, came alongside in his boat, and landed us on his humble quay, where we sank up to our knees in soft mud. Touched by the abject looks of the boatman, I opened my purse and gave him a shilling, being the smallest silver coin I had.

"God of Abram! was ever there such waste?" screamed the Jew. Instead of being thankful, however, the poor boatman looked more abject than before, and, holding the shilling in the palm of his hand, declared, as my companion informed me, that he would prefer the smallest coin of his own country to that which I had given him. The Jew promptly took him at his word, and made an exchange with him of another piece of silver weighing certainly much less than the one I had given the Dutchman.

Our way lay along an apparently interminable straight path, fringed on either side with stunted willows, all of the same age, shape, and height. On the right was a vast marsh or bog; on the left some smooth, even meadows, of a velvet-like softness, cut into square pieces, and intersected by narrow ditches. The morning sky, purified by a strong sea breeze, had worn a silvery brightness, but, as the day wore away, a dense fog suddenly sprang up from the fens and marshes, which, mingling with the warm sunbeams, yielded an intense radiance, blending in broad luminous bars tints of amber, saffron, and gold. In these very meadows Albert Cuyp found the subjects of his rich and glowing pencil. It was milking time, and fat, ruddy girls, bedizened with all manner of strange trinkets, in the form of jewellery, passed to and fro carrying large brass vessels on their heads. My friend stopped and managed to sell them a portion of the more tawdry articles of merchandise which he carried about him. I much enjoyed some of the sweet milk which they proffered us, and regretted that my inexplicable and economical companion prevented my paying for it. We came to a roadside inn, and did a little more business. An English gentleman, one of our fellow-passengers, who had, somehow, also made his way forward, came up, and engaged the Jew as an interpreter. My friend here, also, contrived to make a profit of the stranger's necessities, by changing a sovereign for him at a tolerably good discount. Wherever my friend went he had an eye to business. Taking a barge at Dort, we ran into the mud of Rotterdam about midnight, and, having left the adventurous Englishman at an hotel, where the Jew exacted a small commission for introducing him, we crossed over about forty bridges, and arrived without further hindrance at the Jew's paternal home. We had hit the time to a minute. The widow Lazarus was expecting her son, and was actually boiling a large carp for his supper. She had not beheld her most amiable offspring for a year, yet she displayed no very great excitement. In fact, she hardly raised her eyes as we entered the dim room. A few guttural sounds escaped her aged lips, during the demolition of the carp, which my friend almost consumed without assistance on my part.

CHAPTER LVII.

THE JEW DISCOVERS NEW FEATURES OF CHARACTER.

"WELL, my dear young friend, what are your plans this morning?" exclaimed old Lazarus, as rising from my bed my eyes beheld, through the dull casement of the widow's house, a dingy fragment of the bustling city of Rotterdam.

"I have something in your way, my friend," continued the Jew, without waiting for my answer, "about which I wish to consult you. Here are catalogues of some fine paintings, at an ancient mansion near the Hague, which are to be sold to-morrow and the following day. While breakfast is preparing we will con them over. I have the only two catalogues which reached London. I secured them both from the agent there, in order that the thing might not become known. I will take you to see the paintings, for I mean to buy largely, and shall be glad of your advice. You understand me?"

"Certainly; you want my opinion with respect to the pictures you ought to purchase, and the prices you ought to give for them."

"That is very much like what I mean; you are very near the mark."

"But tell me, where is Signor Bezza," I asked, for this was a point upon which the skilful speculator had volunteered me no further information.

"Not so fast, my impetuous young friend. You will see that gentleman in good time, never fear me. Business before pleasure."

I here ventured to remind my imperious friend, that I had tasted very little pleasure since I had known him, whereupon he abruptly stopped me, and, putting on an injured look, told me that I wronged him; that but for me he might have done better than he had; that the Signor was really living at the Hague, whither he would take me, and that he had planned his morrow's visit to that place partly on my account. To this I made answer that he must excuse me if I had expressed some anxiety about the Signor and his daughter, and added that my confidence in his promises was in no way diminished, and that I would still be ruled by him in all things. I uttered these words in all sincerity, for, indeed, spite of his capriciousness and meanness, there was a power of fascination in old Lazarus to which I irresistibly succumbed. Apparently flattered by my earnest assurance of undiminished confidence, he replied, saying that "I might with some reason charge him with being slow to fulfil his promises, but, after all was said on that score that could be said, what was the loss of a few years to one of my age? Besides, had I not, during the delay, acquired a large amount of invaluable experience of the world?"

"You may smile," he continued; "you have talent —I do not deny it; but I can tell you, were I to withdraw my experience and assistance, you might never find Signor Bezza. Why, how stands the case? At this hour you are a rich man; when you met with the Bezzas in London you were to all intents and purposes a beggar. Formerly you worked hard, and fared anything but sumptuously, I admit; and you will allow that I have fared but indifferently well myself. It may seem strange to you; but I, for my part, prefer this changeful, wandering life to the luxury of palace and chariot. Money I have enough, and more than you suppose; yet, for all I possess, I would not forfeit my word. Not a week has passed since you worked under my roof without my receiving reliable intelligence of the Signor's movements. In fact, he has been nearly all along in my employ, at the Hague. You are one of the last to whom I would act unjustly. I have known you long, before you could well run alone. When on my visits to Madame Mitchel's house, while other children fled affrighted at my presence, you, I well remember it, approached me with confidence, and even with respect. As a boy, during all my dealings with your old master, the carver, you ever treated me with regard: since then you have believed in me, and followed my counsel; I pray you put your faith in me a little longer."

My friend having thus unexpectedly expressed himself, he resumed his usual manner, and proposed that we should not go out empty-handed, but exert ourselves to turn a penny by the way. I agreed to assist him, and he forthwith loaded me with a variety of useful commodities, such as street hawkers usually carry, and which the widow, who seemed to enter into all her son's commercial pursuits, had done up into convenient parcels. Having taken a similar quantity himself, we set out on our journey. I was about to question my companion as to the destination of our store of merchandise, when he began howling or crying the various articles for sale, so as to make the long, narrow street ring from end to end. I found that I was hawking for the first time. We had a capital run of business. The Jew, I noticed, took care to ease his own arms first. At length, just as I was heartily weary, and was thinking of throwing the remains of my stock into the canal, we sold the last lot to a sea-captain, and immediately set out for the place of our destination. Arrived at the old château where the paintings were on view prior to sale, we were soon busied with the Teniérses, Boths, Huysums, Wouvermans, Hondekoeters, and Ostades; scrutinizing and pricing such lots as the Jew thought would suit his market: and having brought this operation to a close, my mission, as far as my friend was concerned, was completed.

On leaving the château, with the view of retracing our steps to the city of the Hague, the Jew took me by the hand in a friendly manner, familiar and altogether different from his usual habit, and, with a kindness of expression I had thought hardly possible in a face so hard and mercenary, he said:

"Hitherto, my young friend, you have only known 'Old Lazarus' as the dealer, as the driver of hard bargains; and seeing him only in that capacity, you can hardly have formed a fair estimate of him: you shall see him to-night under another and more generous aspect. The world I regard as a common stage, on which I am content, in its sight, to play the vulgar parts, varying my cast as it suits me betwixt the pedler, the merchant, and the money-lender. To-night you shall be my guest, and sup with the actor at home."

As we passed along, he paused on the edge of a canal, where a boor was seated near a tubful of live carp and tench, such as one sees depicted in the kitchen scenes of Snyders; and, accosting the fisherman, the Jew selected and bargained for four of the largest and fattest tench.

"Now, my young friend," exclaimed my companion, "go to your lodgings, attire yourself in your smartest raiment, and in an hour's time meet me at yonder mansion with the marble portico. Ask no questions of man or woman by the way, but come as I have bidden you, and fail not, as you love Laura Bezza."

CHAPTER LVIII.

THE JEW'S PLOT.

On our way to the old château where the pictures were on view, prior to their sale, the Jew had stopped at a pleasant little tenement, and engaged lodgings for me. The mistress of the establishment was an Englishwoman who had married early, and settled at the Hague, and where, having lost her husband, she had managed by her own industry to rear her family in respectability. Among other accomplishments, they all spoke tolerable English, which was fortunate for me. On leaving my friend in the fish-market, I hastened to my lodging, and, not suffering any hindrance in making myself understood, I was the more speedily prepared for my appointment at the house on the quay, with the marble portico. I know not what possessed me, but on this occasion I bestowed more pains in dressing than I remember ever to have taken before. All the time I was engaged at the glass, I could not help reverting to the Jew's altered demeanour towards me. By some sort of magic, he had awakened sensations long dormant within my breast, and rekindled my earliest and fondest hopes. The stars lit up the cloudless sky, as I took my solitary way along the dark canal, and over the bridge which led to the mansion the Jew had pointed out, and which, owing to its singularity, could not well be mistaken. I paused at the door, where my ancient friend stood in readiness to receive me. Taking a lamp, he led me into a little office, and, without so much as asking me to be seated, commenced an earnest and animated conversation with a small man bearing the unmistakable characteristics of the Hebrew race.

"Business before pleasure, as usual, you see," cried the Jew, turning to me when the conversation ceased. "It was ever my rule. But come," he added in his late much-improved manner, "now let us go to supper. You have fasted long, and must needs be hungry;" saying which he conducted me up a flight of stone steps, into a large room furnished in a costly manner. In the centre stood a table, on which were preparations for our repast. Seeing me cast an inquiring glance over the apartment, my host interrupted my curiosity, by observing:

"I am expecting a couple of friends to supper, who, if I mistake not, will prove as agreeable to you as to myself. Before, however, I do myself the pleasure of introducing you, I must inflict upon you a little ceremony, which I am afraid will try your patience. When, however, the brief prelude is over, you will not, I am sure, feel ungrateful to me. Anyhow, it is a trifling fancy of mine, which your good-nature will hardly permit you to mar. You will favour me by remaining in this small chamber," pointing to one leading out of that in which we were, "and it is my wish that you leave the door ajar. What I have to say to my friends on their coming, I wish you also to hear."

With these peculiar injunctions, the Jew hand ed me into a side room, carefully closing the door, leaving only a sufficient opening for the purpose he had specified. I had barely seated myself, when footsteps on the stairs announced approaching guests, whom I immediately knew from the way in which my mysterious friend welcomed them.

"Signor," he said, "I am glad to see you and your lovely daughter, and in such good time too. Be seated, I pray, until my repast is in readiness. I know not how it is, Signor, but I never look upon your daughter's handsome face without being reminded of a most noble youth I once met with in Genoa, and about whom, until supper is served, I will tell you a story. Come, if I mistake not, it must be as much as thirty years back. I was myself a mere stripling, some forty years of age or so, but, young as I was, I had the reputation of being trustworthy, so much so that a wealthy uncle, to whom I owed the bread I consumed, was wont to entrust me upon errands of some consequence. On the occasion to which my memory now leads me, I had gone disguised in coarse habiliments to the residence of a titled lady, in order to convey to her a large sum of money in gold, and to receive from her, by way of security, a diamond of huge dimensions and of the first water. Whether it was owing to the greatness of the responsibility, or whether that lady's refulgent charms oppressed my brain, or whether fear of meeting with abuse from the populace, at that time bitter against our race, I cannot now certainly tell; a sort of unconsciousness came over me as I left the palace, and in that state I proceeded on my way. Guess my horror when, on awakening from my trance, I discovered that I had dropped the casket of which I had taken charge, and which contained the third largest and best diamond in Europe! At first I stood still, gazing at my hands, doubting my eyes, and questioning whether the treasure was not still in my grasp. Then was I seized with fear and trembling, as though I had an ague fit. Anon, I howled like one demented, and dashed myself against the stones, rent my clothes and tore my hair by handfuls from my head: and all this took place in the centre of Genoa where I was one of the hated and accursed. In an instant, like the wild waves of the sea, which have broken through their bounds, the mob, which my frantic gestures had attracted, rushed upon me, crying out, "Behold, he is mad! Behold, the mad Jew!" There had been some reason in their cries had they stopped there; but, like all mobs, knowing neither moderation nor humanity, they beat me with sticks and pelted me with dirt, until I sank down upon the earth. Verily I had died upon the spot but for a handsome youth, who, attracted by the noise, came and beat off my cowardly assailants, and carried me bodily off to a place of safety. Such was my despair at the loss of my jewel, that the death from which I had been rescued had not been altogether unwelcome to me. Indeed, as my noble deliverer sat me down, out of harm's way, I barely thanked him. "What has been the cause of all this?" he asked; whereupon I told him of my misfortune and consequent behaviour in the market-place, and described the size and quality of the jewel I had lost. "God be praised!" exclaimed my deliverer, "give yourself no more anxiety;" and taking from his vest the very casket I had dropped, he placed it in my hands, and disappeared before I could recover from my joyful surprise, or learn how or where he came to pick up the casket. Years passed on, but I never forgot the image of that noble youth. It haunted me sleeping or waking, until at last I beheld in this maiden the features I had long sought in vain, and found, moreover, in you the self-same man who so generously restored my gem and so bravely preserved my life."

Signor Bezza, I need hardly say, heard this speech with scarcely less astonishment than myself: but the Jew spoke with so much feeling and volubility that it was impossible for his hearer to reply. I was myself rising from my seat and about to rush forward, but the Jew continued, with increased energy, "Signor Bezza," said he, "I need not remind you of your quarrel with the young Pole at Madame Mitchel's. I had then but recently discovered and identified you as my great friend. It was high time that I made you some return for the gracious service you did me. You will remember how, on that night, I followed in your steps, and how, prompted by my advice and aided by my purse you came here. It was I who employed you (not without profit to myself certainly) since that hour. This night brings our troubles to a close. Your fortune has improved. See, here are no less than a thousand guilders, which my agent has received from the Burgomaster Delt on account of your last five inimitable statuettes. Receive it from my hands without discount, and make note of the fact. It is the first, it may be the last instance of disinterestedness on my part in business matters. Stop! I will just take one per cent. profit, in order to spare *your* feelings and my own at the same time. There, that will do. And now, my young lady, why so dull? Does not your father's good fortune move you to be happy? There was, if I mistake not, one who for long years loved you tenderly—one who for you would toil through life without repining—one who, if it were needed to test his love, would, nay, who *has* to my knowledge braved insult and danger and privations for your sake. Behold he is here, shut up like a jewel in a casket."

For myself, I could scarcely help smiling at finding my kind friend the Jew sticking close to his profession, even in his similes. But the thought was quickly followed by other feelings, as the old man opened wide the door of my room, and led me forward. The effect of this last scene in the Jew's play, I need not say, was most satisfactory.

After we had dried the tears from our eyes—even the Jew was not unmoved—we sat down to supper, during which my now-*venerable* host never ceased to laud my behaviour and my constancy during the time he had known me, and which he said dated back to the period when I first left the cradle—a good-natured testimonial which certainly had the merit of extending over a sufficient period of time.

My eulogist, perhaps because the exercise was new to him, went even further, and compared me to the monster diamond he had lost so tragically in the streets of Genoa.

CHAPTER LIX.

AT HOME AT THE HAGUE.

AFTER a short time spent in preparing a home, I and Laura were married. The English landlady, with whom I lodged, took the responsibility of the details off our hands, and managed matters so well that no accident happened to mar in the smallest degree the happiness of any one concerned.

Our lives pass pleasantly. The days are often varied by short carriage drives, concluding with a repast at which old Lazarus is sometimes present. We have a pretty, small brick house, faced with white stone, on the road that leads to the sea, and so near that in stormy weather the noise of the swelling waves can be distinctly heard as we sit round the polished stove in common use, and to which I am not altogether reconciled.

We have a pleasant window, to which mirrors

are attached in such a manner as to reflect the road up and down, with a distant glimpse of the wide ocean beyond, which is commonly specked with fishing-boats. Occasionally we steal an hour on sunny mornings to stroll on the beach, or into the wood, or the picture gallery, whose walls are covered with masterpieces. But if we have any one more favourite resort than another, it is the wood. We penetrate the intricate lanes formed by the stately trees. It was autumn when we made our first stroll in the wood, and the winds scattered the yellow leaves in showers about our heads and covered the green sward; and here and there, in quiet nooks, ponds of clear, bright water glowed like golden basins under the spreading branches. Musicians came into the principal avenue, and especially a blind girl came thither on that particular morning with her harp, and played and sang most tunefully. We are happy; the Signor was never so happy in his life. He spends fewer hours with Dante, and has taken to the cultivation of tulips for a pastime. He has plenty to do in making designs for jewellery, plate and statuettes, on which, from natural fondness for the work, Laura's hand is sometimes employed. She chases in precious metals to perfection. For myself, I receive as many commissions as I can execute from rich merchants, who are many of them experienced connoisseurs in pictures. I also keep up a correspondence with my old patron the ex-governor, in England. Nor have we forgotten old friends. Altoviti and the print-seller have paid us a visit.

THE END.

CPSIA information can be obtained
at www.ICGtesting.com
Printed in the USA
LVHW040531190122
708837LV00003B/181

9 783752 555363